Tomasito and The Golden Llamas

Tomasito and the Golden Llamas

JANE CASTELLANOS

DECORATIONS BY ROBERT COREY

Golden Gate Junior Books

San Carlos, California

To Alice

Contents

Farewell   3

To Cuzo   11

Don Pedro   23

The Llamas   37

At Sea   47

Harvest   55

The Golden Gate   62

Mountains Again   69

Work   76

Joe   89

School   104

Winter   118

The Broken Idol   128

The Pieces of The Past   140

Tomasito and The Golden Llamas

Farewell

"Ay, Teresa. Will we ever see our ruins again?"

"You will, Tomasito. You will come back from California, with all your learning, to explore them again with Don Pedro. But I? Who knows, my brother, whether I will ever return to Peru." Teresa reached out as if to clasp the mountains in her arms.

The brother and sister stood at the prow of a great cliff which seemed set to sail into the purple shadows of the gorge. Before them the mountain peaks, black against the setting sun, floated like conical islands in a sea of space. Tomasito leaned forward. Far, far below he could still see the tiny snake of the river racing its glittering way along the bottom.

"Come, Tomasito, we must go. It is getting dark. Jack is waiting."

The young boy turned slowly and began to follow his sister down the familiar slope. Her silhouette looked the same as ever —the sturdy, compact form of a young Indian woman in bell-shaped skirts, a blanket sloping from her shoulders, and the gay brim of her Pisac hat curving up like a soup plate. She had taken off the shoes, bought for her wedding, to let her feet feel again the ancient stones of the ruined town.

It was hard for Tomasito to believe that perhaps he would never see her like this again. Tomorrow she would put on her shoes and her city clothes and would start on her way with Señor Jack, to be a North American wife. Tomasito wondered if, in the United States, she would become a different person. He shivered a little. Suppose he too were to change? At least he and Teresa would have each other. But would his sister pay him any mind? For a week now, ever since she had been married to Señor Jack, she had seemed to think of no one but her new husband.

But now, suddenly, Teresa stopped and waited for him. "Look at the stars, Tomasito! The sky is giving a fiesta for us!"

It was true. Tomasito leaned back against a wall and turned his face to the heavens. They were ablaze with lights, like a city strung with lanterns.

"Jack says they have different stars in California. Will they be as beautiful as these?" Teresa wondered.

"Señor Jack thinks so," replied Tomasito.

They continued their way down the slope. As they walked, their hands slipped along the ancient walls, caressing the giant stones which were fitted so smoothly that not even a fingernail could find a crack between them.

Jack must have seen them coming in the starlight. They saw the lights of his car go on. Teresa began to run. Tomasito could see her husband's tall, angular figure coming toward them from out of the shadows.

"Can you find your way home, Tommy?" asked Señor Jack in Spanish. Tomasito was disgusted. He had climbed over the

4

ruins daily for most of his twelve years! He knew them blind-fold. But he only said, "*Si, señor.*"

"We'll come up for you tomorrow then. You still want to go, don't you, son?"

Tomasito didn't dare let himself think about his answer. He just said, "*Si, señor,*" again. He started off in the dark.

"Try to sleep, little one," his sister called after him. Then he heard the car door slam and the motor start and grow fainter around the bend of the road.

Tomasito followed a terrace wall around the side of the mountain. He started to climb again. To the right and left of him rose the black cubicles of stone houses. Most of them showed jagged, roofless gables against the jewelled sky. These were Inca houses, part of the ruined town, still standing, mirac-ulously, after five hundred years.

One or two of the ancient buildings had roofs of thatch and Tomasito could smell fires and hear the small, quiet noises of animals and people making ready for sleep. These were the homes of the workmen hired by the government to keep the ruins cleared of weeds and vines and to look after the tourists who came to see them. Tomasito's father had left his old home in Pisac, up the river, to become one of the guides. In addition, he drove the bus which took tourists from the Government Hotel to the ruins, and he also drove back and forth to the railway station down in the gorge. Teresa had worked at the hotel until she had married Señor Jack. Even Tomasito had sometimes been allowed to take a party of tourists around by himself.

Tomasito stopped beside a wall. His hand pressed a familiar latch. The starlight illuminated a courtyard between two build-ings. The building on the left showed a faint line of light. From its roof a column of smoke wavered through the thatch. Tomasi-

5

to pushed open the rough wooden door and entered the kitchen.

The scene was so familiar and unchanging that the boy could scarcely believe this would be the last time he would be a part of it. Domitila, his fourteen-year-old sister, was stirring the stew boiling on the clay stove. Papá, squatting on his heels, was drinking a glass of chicha. He turned to smile at Tomasito. Jacinto, six, and Rosita, seven, were feeding the squealing guinea pigs in their stone trough along the wall of the room. The air was heavy with the spicy steam of the stew and with the smoke which missed the opening in the thatch above the clay stove. On all sides the strong stone walls of the Incas kept them safe and warm.

Tomasito squatted next to his father on the hard earthen floor. The sight of Domitila's gourd scooping into the pot and rising again with its fragrant load usually made him unbearably hungry. But tonight he watched as in a dream. When his sister handed him his own bowl he ate mechanically, thinking of tomorrow. Tomasito knew that his father was sad too, but neither dared to speak. The younger children had finished with the guinea pigs and were now sitting on the floor with their own bowls of stew. Domitila had finally left her work in order to eat.

Rosita and Jacinto ate and talked with enthusiasm. To them, Tomasito and Teresa's trip to North America was no more dismaying than the departure of their older brother, Pablo, to work in the mines. They expected Tomasito and Teresa to come back, as he did, for the Christmas fiestas, bringing them gifts and tales of adventure. They babbled freely between mouthfuls, clicking along in Quechua, the language of their Inca ancestors.

"Will you bring a husband from the United States for Domitila?" asked Rosita. After all, Pablo had brought his friend Señor

6

Jack, from the mines, to visit and Señor Jack had married Teresa.

"Domitila will probably marry long before I return," replied Tomasito. The children looked startled. For as long as they could remember, Domitila and, before her, Teresa, had cooked and washed and cared for them. Their mamá had died soon after Jacinto's birth.

"Then who will take care of us?" asked Jacinto, in his anxiety forgetting the excitement over Tomasito's departure.

"Don't worry, little one," comforted Domitila. "I'll not go to North America!" There was a trace of acid in her tone. "And I would take care of you even if I *did* get married—that is, until Rosita can cook all by herself."

"Rosita cook?" Jacinto started to tease.

His father said quietly, "No, I cannot spare any more of my children. Too many will be gone. But Pablo may come back if he gets a job on the railroad. And Tomasito will come back, too, when he is grown, to tell us about the United States and to study at the University."

"Tomasito, will you bring our llamas back with you when you come?" asked Jacinto.

"No," replied Tomasito. "They are Jack's llamas now. I am only going to take care of them for him."

"But why does Señor Jack have to take our llamas? Why doesn't he get some in North America?"

"They don't have llamas in the United States," replied his father. "Except in cages for people to look at. In California Señor Jack is going to let the children look at our llamas and ride on them as well. The children's parents will pay for the rides and Señor Jack and Teresa will earn some money."

"But why can't Señor Jack work in the mines in California so that he won't have to earn money with our llamas?" Rosita

7

inquired sadly. "I love Puca and Kuzni and Allca and Quilla! I don't want them to stay in the United States!"

"I know, my daughter," answered her father. "We shall all miss our little animals. But the money from the llama rides will help pay for Tomasito's food. That way he can stay in North America and study to pass his examinations. When he comes back he will have the money Señor Jack gave me for the llamas to use at the University."

But all this seemed very confusing to Rosita and Jacinto and they looked woebegone.

"Time to sleep now," ordered Domitila, putting the children's bowls on the table. She shepherded them out the door and across the starry courtyard to the building on the far side.

Tomasito and his father stood up too. "Father, I must say good-by to our other llamas before I go to sleep."

"Good, my son. The little animals will miss you. But I am glad that you will be there to take care of the others." Papá rested his hand a moment on his son's shoulder.

"Good night, my father."

Tomasito found his way to the street and turned to the right. Next to the Inca house the family used for a kitchen was another building which had been thatched to serve as a barn. It had no wooden door and, like the other houses, was window-less. It was dark inside after the starlight outdoors but here and there a star pricked through the roof where the thatch had become thin.

The boy knew where each llama was accustomed to sleep. There were only three of them left now. The four sold to Señor Jack were already on their way to Cuzco. After Teresa's wedding Pablo had driven them as far as Pisac, on his way back to the mines. Tío Dominguez, an elderly relative of Papá's, would

drive them the rest of the way. Señor Jack, Teresa, and Tomasito would meet the old man in Cuzco.

Like so many Indians, Tomasito was deeply attached to his
animals. The other families working at the ruins had left their
llama herds behind in their native villages, but Papá had persuaded the government that it would please the tourists to take
pictures of these exotic creatures grazing on the slopes and
terraces of the ancient city—which, of course, it did. So Papá's
llamas had come with him from Pisac and had remained as part
of the family.

Tomasito knew that his father had hesitated many weeks
before deciding to sell four of the beloved creatures to Señor
Jack. It was only to give Tomasito a chance to go to the
University that he had been willing to do so.

With the four gone, the barn seemed full of night. Tomasito
went to each llama, stroked its coarse wool all over, and put his
arms around each woolly neck.

"I shall come back, Blackie," he whispered. "And Cloud, you
will have little ones, to take the place of your friends in North
America. When I come back they will already be grown, grazing on the terraces with Jacinto. Good-by, dear golden one. I
shall remember you shining in the sun, like the llamas of the
Golden Enclosure."

The three llamas, silent and unseen in the night, gave no sign
that they had heard. But in the mind of the young boy, who had
conversed for years with his animal friends, there was no doubt
that they understood. As a child no older than Jacinto, he had
begun to accompany Domitila when she took the herd to pasture on the steep slopes. Boy and beasts had developed a silent
language which went beyond the almost inaudible clicks and
whistles with which Tomasito guided their movements on the
path ahead of him.

"I shall pray that I may become a good student. Then I can come back soon and make you and Papá proud," whispered the boy from the doorway. Perhaps he was right. Perhaps three delicate heads did turn toward him in the darkness, to bid him farewell.

To Cuzco

THAT NIGHT Tomasito dreamed that he was in the United States. Señor Jack had taken him to the zoo in San Francisco. Presently they came to a sign which read, "To the Llamas." As they turned the corner their eyes were dazzled by the sheen of a garden made of gold. Trees and flowers, birds, deer, and rows of corn plants—in perfect detail all were wrought in gold.

"It is the Golden Enclosure of the Incas," exclaimed Tomasito in his dream. "But there are no llamas!" As he said this, Kuzni and Puca and Allca and Quilla, who had been solemnly preceding Tomasito and Señor Jack along the pathways of the park, suddenly began to enter the gateway of the Golden Enclosure. Tomasito watched in horror as each llama took his place in the Golden Garden—to become immobilized, a perfect golden llama!

"Señor Jack! I must save them!" shouted Tomasito. He dashed forward to enter the gateway.

"No! No! Tomasito, come back!" Señor Jack lunged after him,

caught him by one arm and pulled him outside. He was safe. But his hand felt numb and heavy. He looked down. The hand which had touched the gate had turned to gold.

"Tomasito! Wake up!" Domitila's voice called. He opened his eyes. But it was difficult to believe that he was really awake for his hand felt lifeless. Fearfully he raised it, half expecting it to be made of gold. What a relief to see that it was red and wrinkled from being slept on!

The light from the open door revealed that Domitila had brought over from the kitchen a bowl of water, and had laid out the new clothes which had been bought for him in Pisac. Papá had already gone out. Tomasito's heart began to race with excitement. The day of departure had finally arrived!

Tomasito had tried on his new clothes in the store in Pisac, but at the time he had not really recognized the image facing him in the mirror. Today, too, the figure that looked back at him from Domitila's looking-glass did not seem real—a boy in his own image but with strange clothes, as if he had somehow got mixed up with Pablo or Señor Jack. However, the sight was pleasant, if eerie, and he began to be impatient for Jack and Teresa to come.

Tomasito could not have told whether or not he managed to eat breakfast. He was only half aware of Domitila's maternal cluckings and the squealing of the guinea pigs. The younger children ate in unaccustomed silence and looked at him over their bowls with large eyes.

"Señor Jack!" Jacinto was the first to hear the sound of the car outside. All four abandoned breakfast and rushed out into the courtyard. By the time they had opened the gate the hotel station wagon had stopped at the foot of the street and Jack was getting out. Like cats, the children and Domitila ran in their bare feet down the steep stone street, but Tomasito, in his heavy new shoes, found it hard not to slip on the cobblestones.

"Come up front with us, Tommy," said Señor Jack. Tomasito climbed in next to his father, who was driving. Señor Jack installed the children in their favorite rear seat. Domitila, in pigtails and Indian dress, glanced shyly at her sister sitting next to her in the middle seat. Teresa looked for all the world like the tourist ladies from Lima or the United States, even to a shiny new handbag.

"No trouble starting the car, at any rate," laughed Señor Jack. Papá released the brake and let the motor start as the car rolled into the steep curve. Below them one angular turn after another zigzagged down the side of the gorge. Señor Jack and Papá joked about the tourists, who were invariably frozen with terror at the sight below them. They passed the Government Hotel but did not stop as, fortunately on this important morning, there were no tourists wanting to take the Cuzco train.

As they descended into the gorge the sharp mountain air became soft and warm. They drove through luminous clouds of mist which were rising from the distant river, as if the river itself were boiling into steam. The plants along the side of the road became more luxuriant—orchids, yellow calciolarias, begonias, and crimson fuchsias dripped from the leafy walls.

At last the road reached the frothing river and Papá drove the station wagon onto the steel bridge. In a few minutes they were at the station on the far side. Indian women, in turquoise and sapphire skirts and white felt hats, had already gathered, babies cradled in the carrying blankets across their backs. Men of the maintenance crew, railroad officials, and small boys added to the throng. None of these people were going to ride on the train but every day they congregated here for the pleasure of seeing it appear and disappear.

"It's coming!" squealed Rosita. She and Jacinto leaned so far

13

over the track that Domitila barely snatched them back in time as the single yellow car (a bus, actually, which ran on tracks) slid to a halt before the station.

"Say good-by now," Papá said to the children. "Then go with Domitila to the car."

Rosita and Jacinto were suddenly very quiet. They stood awkwardly while Señor Jack patted them on the head. They looked dumbly at Tomasito who stared back dazedly. They hid their faces in Teresa's strange skirt as she tried to hug them and Domitila at the same time.

Papá and Señor Jack had put the new family's luggage into the yellow car. A whistle blew, voices called, and somehow Tomasito found himself hustled up the metal steps and into a seat near the window. Teresa sat down beside him. Papá was standing at the door of the car. His face looked very still. "Good-by, my children," he called. "God keep you."

Suddenly the doors closed and Papá seemed to slide backward, becoming smaller and somehow lonely looking as the train clicked gently on through the gorge.

Although his older brother and sisters had made the trip to Cuzco, Tomasito had never been on the car which he had watched so often from the station. At first he felt a little confused as the leafy walls rushed past the windows. Since the sides of the gorge were so steep, the roof of the car cut off the sky. It seemed as if they were being pulled through a green tunnel. The river on the left, in reality racing furiously toward the jungle, seemed to be getting nowhere, seething in stationary rage.

Teresa began to point out to him the homes of people who had come to the station or whom they had met at the market town. Jack, who sat across the aisle from them, began to converse in Spanish with the other two occupants of the car. One of

14

these, an Inspector of Ancient Monuments for the government, was returning to his home in Cuzco after a trip down the river. The second man, Father Graña, a priest from a mission on the Amazon, was reporting to his order in Lima.

Señor Lorca, the government official, and Father Graña told of life on the great jungle rivers. This land of dense forests, strange animals, and people whom even the Inca warriors had had to respect, was also part of Peru. But how different from the lofty peaks of Tomasito's home and the high, bare plains which Jack and Pablo had described.

Jack was telling the Peruvians of his amazement at sight of the breathtaking sweep of the Andes when he had first seen them during shore leave from an American naval ship. He had promised himself, he said, that after his tour of duty ended he would come back to explore those snowy spaces which were even grander than the Sierra of his own homeland.

Tomasito already knew the story of how Jack had gotten himself a job as an electrician in the American mines at Cerro de Pasco, and, with his new Peruvian friends, had explored the high plateaus, dazzling slopes, and the mysterious ruins of the ancient empire of the Incas. It was just such an expedition which had brought him, with Pablo, to visit their own beloved ruins.

"This is my friend, Jack McGerraghty, from the United States," Pablo had announced one day when the family met him at the station at the beginning of one of his holiday leaves. "He works with me at the mine. I am going to show him our ruins."

Jack had been astonished by their ruins. "*Díos mío!* How did they ever do it? It would take us millions of dollars worth of machinery to build a city on a peak like this—and I wouldn't want to bet that it would last five hundred years."

But what had impressed Jack even more had been Teresa.

15

"You didn't tell me the ruins were still inhabited by beautiful girls!" he teased Pablo. Jack was staying at the hotel and Teresa had been working there. When Pablo would stop by to take his friend on a tour of the ancient buildings he would have a hard time prying him loose from the breakfast table. Jack would laugh and say, "They should let the girls be the guides. Then you'd see how fast I'd get ready!"

After that first vacation Jack had come back several times "to visit the ruins." Finally, when it was time for him to return to the United States, he had asked Papá for permission to marry Teresa. Papá hated to let one of his daughters go so far away, but he could see that Jack would take good care of her. And then Jack had offered to take Tomasito with them so that he could study and eventually enter the University.

"You are going back to the mines, Señor?" the Inspector asked now.

"No, the time has come when I must return to my home country," replied Jack. "I am on my way to the Sierra of California."

"You will work in the mines in California?" inquired the priest.

"No. My brother has started an electrical contracting business. He wants me to go in with him. Even our mountains are building up fast. Hope I can stand the crowds!" Jack laughed.

"But I had to take a little bit of Peru with me," he continued affectionately. "This is my wife, Teresa, and my brother-in-law, Tomasito Chavez." Teresa and Tomasito smiled shyly as the men nodded to them.

"And what will you do in the United States, my son?" the priest asked Tomasito.

"I am going to school, Father, to study English and history and mathematics and science," Tomasito answered.

16

"Good, my son. But I hope that you will not forget our Peru."

"Oh, no, Father! When I have learned enough to take my examinations, I am coming back to the University in Cuzco. Don Pedro said I could learn to be an archeologist and help him discover more of the lost cities of the Incas."

"Ah, you know Don Pedro Guzman!" exclaimed Father Graña. "One of the great scholars of Peru! It would indeed be an honor to work with him."

Tomasito felt very embarrassed at having attracted so much attention and was glad when the Inspector called out that they were approaching Ollantay-Tambo.

"If you look carefully," he explained, "you can see the foundations of the ancient Inca bridge. See—over there!"

Tomasito looked eagerly out the window. His friend Don Pedro had told him about this famous bridge, one of a series of bridges woven so skillfully of cactus fibers and attached so securely to stone piers that for hundreds of years the soldiers and nobles of the Lord Inca, and even the Spaniards with their horses, had passed safely over raging mountain torrents on its swaying strands. All that could be seen now was the base of the stone towers that had held the ropes.

Fortunately, the train was to stop for a few minutes at Ollantay, so Jack said they might walk about on the platform. Tomasito was able to get a quick look at the town. It was literally carved into the steep walls of the gorge. For lack of other space modern houses had been built on the foundations of the Inca town. Indians of four hundred years ago had walked the same streets as the Ollantayans of today. They had looked up at the same terraced fields and at the same fortress crowning the rim of the canyon. Tomasito felt a little dizzy as his eyes traveled up the vertical side of the gorge. Don Pedro had said that someday he and Tomasito might explore together the ruins of Ollantay.

17

Tomasito could imagine himself with Don Pedro on those breathtaking heights, carefully scraping away vines and dirt from the beautifully fitted stones—finding beneath the trailing stems and wind-blown sand an opening and then a room!

The room he and Don Pedro had dug out near his home had been empty of all except darkness and mystery, but once, the archeologist had told him, he had uncovered a tomb in which a mummy, wrapped in the traces of its tapestry robes and decorated with golden ornaments, lay in its finery like a royal doll. Tomasito would be happy to unearth even the bones of an ancestor of his own—perhaps a weaver of bridges or a messenger of the Lord Inca who had run like the vicuña from fortress to fortress along the sacred river.

Tomasito had pleased Don Pedro because he was willing to dig and scrape and sift day after day, even when they found only more stone walls like the ones they knew or even nothing at all.

"Ah, my son," he had said to the boy one day, "you will indeed make a good archeologist. It is the search you love more than the treasure! An archeologist must first of all be patient, patient, patient. He must always think in terms of centuries, of the hundreds of years of wind and sand and vegetation which have tried to erase the messages from the past!"

And so the two had become fast friends, the famous archeologist, sent by the government to uncover the secrets of the ruins, and the young Indian boy who knew them by heart from years of playing in their stony chambers and herding his llamas on their broad terraces. Don Pedro told the boy story after story of the glorious Empire until the ruins seemed to be peopled with tasseled warriors and the beautiful Virgins of the Sun. He took Tomasito to his room in the hotel and showed him books and photographs of others ruins, of the treasures of the past uncovered all over Peru and in countries throughout the world.

As Tomasito stood now on the station platform at Ollantay, only a few miles from Cuzco, he wished more than anything else that he might visit his famous friend to say good-by before he set off for North America. But he knew that it would hardly be proper for a twelve-year-old boy to suggest plans to a man like Jack, much less to intrude upon a famous scientist.

Just as if his thoughts had flown through the air, Father Graña asked, "Will you see your friend Don Pedro in Cuzco, my son?"

"Oh, Father, I would love so much to see him! But he doesn't know that we are to spend a day there. And I wouldn't dare interrupt him in his work."

"Of course, my son, it would not be right to disturb him. But I am sure that if Don Pedro has asked you to work with him he would like to see you. Perhaps I can help you. I have here in my bag a very interesting relic which I discovered one day in the garden of our school in the jungle. I should like to turn it over to Don Pedro for study. Would you like to go with me when I take it to him?"

Tomasito's gentle, oval face, usually as quiet as a polished stone, became a picture of joy. "Oh, Father, please, yes," he breathed. "Thank you! But first I must ask Señor Jack."

Tomasito had not noticed that Jack and Teresa had left the platform and had entered the Ollantay station. After a brief search he found them, listening somewhat tensely to the station-master. The latter, a small man, buttoned tightly into his uniform, was speaking solemnly. The twinkle in his eye, however, seemed to indicate a certain relish of the effect his words were having upon the passengers.

"An earthquake! Well, what do you know!" exclaimed Jack.

19

"I guess we didn't feel it because we were in motion. Did it dislocate the track?"

"We don't think so, *señor*," answered the stationmaster. "The crew at Cancha spoke of a small slide—some boulders on the track. I think they'll have it cleared in a few hours."

"Perhaps we can have dinner here then, while we're waiting." Jack turned to Teresa and Tomasito. "I know Tommy is hungry. Aren't you, Tommy?"

Tomasito had been standing quietly by his sister while the two men talked. He had been so excited at the prospect of visiting Don Pedro that he had not thought much about food. But now, come to think of it, he was famished!

"*Sí, señor!*" He grinned broadly at Jack whose face—long, bony, and lighted by sky-blue eyes—always looked down at him from what seemed such an astonishing height. Tomasito was too shy to ask him about Don Pedro. Perhaps at dinner—

Fortunately, Father Graña was invited to eat with them, together with Señor Lorca, and the arrangements which the young boy found so difficult to propose were easily taken care of by the priest. It was decided that Tomasito would accompany Father Graña, if Don Pedro permitted, while Jack and Teresa went to meet Tío Dominguez and the llamas. The old man should be arriving from Pisac if all had gone according to plan.

Now it was the arrival in Cuzco which occupied Tomasito's busy mind. As the car finally started off, he was scarcely aware of the discussion of the landslide or of the car's eventual climb out of the valley of the Urubamba River into the high country near Cuzco. He kept thinking of the coming meeting with his old friend. Would Don Pedro really be glad to see him? Had he really meant it when he had said he would make Tomasito his assistant some day? Or had this been his own imagining, like the fantasies with which he had often entertained himself as he herded the llamas?

Tomasito also thought of Cuzco, the Sacred City of the Incas. In a few minutes he would set eyes upon it, as if he were a messenger or an honored official from the provinces, coming for the first time to the City of the Sun. He quite forgot that Don Pedro had told him that the Inca city had been destroyed by the Spaniards. He fully expected to see palaces plated with gold and silver blazing in the setting sun, the temple roofs sparkling with golden thatch.

So it really was a shock, as the car came out on the ridge above the city, to look down and see what appeared to be a gigantic violet bowl, paved with pink tile instead of golden thatch. Although Tomasito had never seen so many roofs in his life, he still felt as though the earthquake had shaken his dreams into collapse.

All the grownups seemed greatly excited for him and exclaimed, "See! Cuzco! Cuzco, Tommy!" It was only Teresa who noticed how tightly he pressed his face to the glass so that Jack would not see how disappointed he was. After a while she moved close to him and asked softly in Quechua, "What is the matter, my brother? Did you expect something different?"

"Where are the palaces of the Lord Inca and the temples plated with gold?" asked Tomasito.

"Ah, those were all destroyed by the Spaniards. Don't you remember? The gold was melted down and carried off across the sea. But don't be sad, Tomasito. The city will seem more beautiful when you get down into it. Look over there. Now you can see the Great Plaza and the fine churches around it. They are splendid when you get close to them. And over there, on the mountain, is the great fortress of Sacshuáman Don Pedro told

21

you about. There are still many wonderful sights in Cuzco. It is still a great city."

Tomasito felt little comfort. But when they stepped out onto the platform of the Cuzco station a new wave of hope lifted his spirits. For the air was alive with delicious music. The bells of Cuzco were pouring into the evening a silver melody that told him not all beauty had died with the Lord Inca.

Don Pedro

TOMASITO was awakened the next morning by the same lovely sounds from the bells. However, one bell was almost deafening in its resonance. The boy leaned out the window of his hotel room to see a large church so close that he could watch its bells rocking in the tower.

Now that he had overcome his early disappointment, it was fascinating to watch the life of a modern city. Naturally, Don Pedro had not thought to describe to him the giant trucks, buses, and automobiles of all sorts which squeezed through the narrow canyons of the streets, stopping and starting with magic regularity. Such sights were fully as astonishing to Tomasito as would have been the processions of the Incas. The stores along the street, with their glittering display windows, reminded him more of what Don Pedro had told him of the storehouses of the Lord Inca than they did of the small shops in Pisac, the largest town of his acquaintance.

Later, after breakfast in the hotel dining room, it seemed to

23

Tomasito that Father Graña would never come to report on the proposed visit to Don Pedro. Jack's and Teresa's conversation, as they waited in the hotel lobby, dealt with his beloved llamas. Listening to it was all that prevented Tomasito from forgetting his manners and running nervously to the front door of the hotel.

Jack and Teresa were to go that day to the outskirts of the city where, presumably, Tío Dominguez had brought the llamas after herding them down from Pisac. A friend had a small house and corral there where they were to have spent the night. Jack was feeling somewhat uneasy for of course there had been no way to get in touch with Tío Dominguez to know whether he had started from Pisac and had arrived safely in Cuzco. Tío Dominguez was very old and quite unimpressed by the passage of time. If they could not get the llamas across town and onto a freight train leaving Cuzco that night, the animals would miss connections with the freighter in Callao which was to take them all to California. Complicated schedules of this sort were unfamiliar to Tomasito and Teresa and they could not quite grasp the necessity for such close timing. But they caught the urgency of Jack's mood and felt uneasy themselves.

At last Father Graña, accompanied by Señor Lorca, entered the hotel lobby. They rose to greet the two men.

"I spoke to Don Pedro last night on the telephone," announced the priest. "He told me to tell Tomasito how very happy he would be to see him. He has made an appointment with me for this morning, to look at my relic and to talk with Señor Lorca and me about explorations in the jungle. But he would like Tomasito to spend the day with him at the University. Is that agreeable, Señor McGerraghty?"

Tomasito's face was ablaze with joy as he saw the smile of assent on Jack's face. It was arranged that Jack and Teresa pick up Tomasito at the University in the late afternoon.

"Good-by, Tommy," Jack said to the boy. "We'll take you along when we load the animals into the train. We'll really need you for that."

"The University is not far," said Father Graña as they left the hotel. He and Señor Lorca strode along, turning occasionally to point out to Tomasito some landmark or other. The boy could not resist stopping every now and then to gaze at the lavishly stocked shop windows. But whenever he did so he would find himself separated from Father Graña by other pedestrians and would have to scurry to catch up.

At last the street ended in a huge plaza. In the center were flowers and a beautiful fountain. On each of the four sides of the plaza was a church, each ornamented with cupolas and elaborate carvings. The churches were quite different from the massive, square church in Pisac, which seemed to belong with the stone cubicles of the town. As Tomasito looked around at the imposing scene he could see that Teresa had been right. Here on the Great Plaza he admitted to himself that Cuzco was still a beautiful and regal city.

Father Graña told him the names of the churches. "And here," he said, turning in at a colonnaded building flanking one of them, "is the University."

At first, the University seemed to consist mostly of long dark tunnels and arcaded courts. Now and again they would come upon a group of young men and women talking together in a hallway. Tomasito would catch a glimpse of a lecture hall, its benches arranged in tiers up the sides of the room like Inca terraces.

Finally the two men walked more slowly and began to look at signs lettered on the yellowed glass of the doors along the corridor.

25

"Instituto de Arqueología," read Father Graña. "This must be it. Ah, here is his office." And he opened a door upon which was lettered, "Doctor Pedro Guzman, *Profesor de arqueología.*"

Before his secretary could announce the visitors, Don Pedro himself opened the door to his inner office and welcomed them in. He greeted Father Graña and Señor Lorca with formal courtesy but he grasped the young boy by the shoulders and gazed at him with warm affection.

"God did not give me a son," he said to the priest, "but he sent this fine young student to comfort and work with me!" Tomasito, overcome with pride and embarrassment, did not know whether to look at Don Pedro or the floor.

"Let's see your relic, Father," invited Don Pedro presently. Father Graña placed a small canvas bag on Don Pedro's desk and pulled from it a heavy roundish object. Don Pedro began unwrapping the layers of newspaper in which it was wrapped.

Tomasito feasted his eyes on his friend as the archeologist, absorbed, bent over a beloved task. Don Pedro was a man of about fifty, somewhat taller than the Indian men of Tomasito's acquaintance, lean and delicate of build. His face was brown from many hours in the sun, but it was long and narrow with a fine mustache. Tomasito loved to watch Don Pedro's hands, brushing the surface of some newly discovered object. His slender fingers moved with the utmost suppleness and delicacy. He looked now a little like the doctor at the government clinic for he wore a white cotton coat over his dark suit.

Don Pedro held Father Graña's stone object in his hand, turning it this way and that and finally examining its surface with a jeweller's eye-piece.

"You are right, Father," Don Pedro said at last. "It does appear to be an Inca mace-head. See, it looks very similar to this one." He took something which looked like a stone flower with six petals from one of the shelves near his desk and placed it near Father Graña's discovery.

"You can certainly see why they find so many broken Inca skulls," remarked Señor Lorca. "I wouldn't want to get hit with that!"

"It is surprising to have found it so far east in the jungle," observed Don Pedro. "As you know, the Incas were not thought to have penetrated that far. It could, of course, have been carried east by jungle Indians traveling along the river. If you would be willing to leave it here, Father, we will study it and see if we can tell when it was made and perhaps even when it was moved."

"Is there any serious possibility, Don Pedro, that the government would plan for excavations that far into the jungle?" asked Señor Lorca.

"It's not very probable," replied Don Pedro. "This was no doubt picked up by some jungle Indian in territory invaded by the Incas. It would be very interesting to make a few exploratory diggings in Father Graña's garden. If you should find one of those crushed skulls there, then we would really have something to think about!"

"And now, Señor Lorca, I have a request to make of you," continued Don Pedro. The latter opened his desk drawer and brought out a tiny clay llama. "As you know, this is an Inca relic. These little llamas were buried in the fields to bring abundant crops. They are found quite commonly, but I know that the government does not want archeological objects removed from the country. Do you think, though, Señor Lorca, that we might obtain permission for Tomasito to take this with him to California—if he brings it back when he returns? I think it might remind him of the treasures of his homeland."

"I am sure, Don Pedro, that the government would not mind

27

in this case. In fact, I will take it upon myself to make sure that the permission is granted," offered the Inspector.

After a cordial exchange of farewells, the priest and Señor Lorca departed and Tomasito was left alone with Don Pedro.

"Come, my son," invited the archeologist. "Let me show you where you may work someday." Tomasito followed his friend through the dark corridors to long dusty rooms where assistants and students were examining, brushing, measuring, and labelling objects which had been brought in from the diggings. Some were carefully gluing small pieces of pottery or statuary. In a shed nearby were crates with larger objects as well as boxes of soil from which tiny bits of pottery or beads or bone were to be sifted.

"You see," said Don Pedro, "we need very patient people to work here. Even the soil clinging to the grooves in a tool or piece of statuary may tell us where it was made and what journeys it took before being buried where we found it. In this way we can follow the travels of the people who made and used it and can begin to piece together their history. Now come into the museum and see what our finds look like when we have finished working on them."

They went next into a long room lined with glass cases in which the objects which the students had prepared were displayed. Here there was no dust. The stone and metal implements, pottery, pieces of fabric and jewelry were polished and set on shining glass shelves. They were arranged in categories so that, as Tomasito walked along, he could imagine the ancient Indians as they lived different aspects of their lives—preparing their food or hunting; or healing the sick with gold and silver instruments; or worshipping the sun in garments of finest wool, decorated with feathers and golden bangles. In one corner of the hall was a fragment of stone wall.

"We had to move that all in one piece," explained Don Pedro. "There are no stone masons today who can lock stones together like that. Fortunately, we did not have to move it far as Cuzco is full of fine stone work. We are collecting materials here to place in a new national museum which will help to teach us all the glorious history of our country."

Tomasito would like to have gone back to the laboratory to watch the assistants at work, but Don Pedro suggested that they go out into the town.

"Yesterday's earthquake," the archeologist told him, "damaged an old house which had been built over four centuries ago on the foundations of an Inca building. Part of the house will have to be torn down and the owner wants to know if the Institute would care to examine the Inca site. Would you like to come with me to have a look at it?"

Of course Tomasito was enchanted to be "working" with Don Pedro again. He was very glad, though, that young boys were not expected to say much to grownups, for the astonishing new sights around him occupied his total attention and left no surplus energy for the use of his tongue.

As they stepped out upon the square Don Pedro reminded Tomasito that this had once been the great ceremonial plaza of the Inca capitol.

"In the days of the Incas, Tomasito," he recounted, "this was called the Huaycapata, the Square of Joy. Imagine it surrounded by huge stone palaces of the Emperors, built of intricate masonry, like the temples near your home, but actually plated with bands and sheets of shining gold. From this point stretched the four royal roads which bound together the four quarters of the enormous empire of the Incas.

"Imagine how this square must have looked during the great festival of Hatun Raimi," he continued as they walked along.

29

"The Lord Inca and his queen were seated on thrones decorated with gold and covered with precious robes. The resplendent mummies of dead Inca emperors and their life-size gold statues were paraded before the Altar to the Sun. The square was filled with nobles and dignitaries dressed in the vivid costumes of their tribes from all over the realm. The air was filled with music and singing and, at the end, the dancers seized the gold-plated cable with scarlet tassels which encircled the plaza, danced with it as with a dazzling serpent, and left it coiled like a sleeping snake on the great plaza!"

Don Pedro himself seemed almost transported as he talked. Tomasito who, in his mind, had been dancing on the plaza, grew sad as the vivid words faded away.

"And is nothing left, Don Pedro? Was everything broken, melted, and carried away by the Spaniards?"

"Almost all, alas!" replied Don Pedro. "They say the Indians threw the golden cable into Lake Urcos. Some say the Indians buried much of their treasure. And some of it has been found, as I have told you. But perhaps you and I will find even more—possibly even under the house to which we are going."

"And the Curi-cancha, the Golden Enclosure, where was it? Was it completely destroyed too?"

"Come, my son, I'll drive you past its site on our way." And Don Pedro motioned Tomasito to a small car parked near the University. A few blocks to the southeast of the great plaza he stopped opposite a church.

"This is the Church of Santo Domingo, Tomasito. Do you notice anything strange about it?"

Tomasito looked at a huge wall of fitted stone blocks surmounted by a Spanish bell tower.

"Sí, señor. It has Inca walls!" exclaimed Tomasito.

"Good! Good! You are learning to be a good archeologist. The

30

Inca walls that you see as part of Santo Domingo were part of the wall of the Golden Enclosure. The Spaniards who saw the Curi-cancha before it was destroyed said that it was as long as a city block, with doors of gold and silver. Inside were temples to the sun, moon, stars, and lightning, and in the middle a fountain encased in gold. Of course you know of the most miraculous part of all—the Golden Garden in which eleven life-size llamas of pure gold grazed on blades of golden grass!"

"Oh, *señor*, how I wish I might have seen that glorious sight!"

"It was indeed a splendid creation. But few of the Indian boys of those days were able to see it either. No one was allowed to travel on the Royal Road, except the Lord Inca, his armies, and his messengers. Most people spent their lives in working day after day in the villages where they were born. Even my ancestor, an Inca princess who married a Spaniard, probably would never have gotten to see the Golden Enclosure. But all of us can go into the church which is here now. Come, let me show you."

Inside the church the candles, gleaming ornaments, and statues were more magnificent than anything Tomasito had ever seen. He was awed by their splendor and by the atmosphere of holiness which filled the lofty spaces of the church. He knew that what Don Pedro meant to say was, "You see, the Spaniards too have given our country beautiful and sacred treasures."

But Tomasito was somehow not content. He still felt, almost as if he had witnessed it, the destruction of the precious Field of the Sun, in which its life-giving rays, immobilized in the metallic landscape, had been extinguished by the invaders.

Tomasito even felt a certain resentment against his friend. It seemed to him that Don Pedro was trying to dilute his righteous anger against the treacherous conquerors of his people, the greedy Spaniards who had not been content with the sheets of solid gold plating the walls, but had melted into crude lumps the delicate petals of the golden flowers and the fleece of the sacred llamas. An ugly thought crossed his mind. "No wonder— Don Pedro is a Spaniard too!"

Tomasito feared that this disturbing and traitorous thought showed in his face, but Don Pedro appeared as gracious and kindly as ever. When they reached the house they were to inspect, the archeologist introduced him affectionately to its owner, Don Joaquin Calancha. The latter greeted his two visitors in a long room lined with polished wood and gilded mirrors. Portraits of gentlemen in velvet coats and lace collars and beautiful women in satin and jewels adorned the walls. Chairs which could have served as thrones stood on either side of the fireplace.

Through his astonishment, Tomasito heard Don Pedro say, "This house, Tomasito, is one of the historical treasures of Cuzco. Don Joaquin's family has occupied it for four hundred years and someday it will become a national monument."

Again, Tomasito felt a wave of anger. So! Another Spaniard. A palace built with Inca gold! But he tried, for Don Pedro's sake, to prevent any of these rude and hostile thoughts from ruffling the serenity of his face.

Don Joaquin was a small, sharp man, all points and glitter. His intense black eyes shone like obsidian and his pointed silver goatee stabbed the air as he talked. His neat, birdlike body seemed to hop about, while his tapered fingers pointed, shook, admonished, accentuating the crispness of his words.

To the boy's surprise, Don Joaquin appeared quite curious about him—his home in the ruins, his father's family in Pisac, and his trip to California. Don Joaquin, it seemed, was quite familiar with the little mountain towns and with the Indians there. Indeed, he seemed even to remember Tío Dominguez, a dignitary of Pisac. But he did not approve very highly of Tomasito's plans for living in the United States.

"That's no place for an Indian," he said, cocking his head to one side. "The Indians there have done nothing for themselves. They have let themselves be pushed back into reservations and ghettos, aren't even treated as citizens!"

Tomasito was beginning to look alarmed. Catching the expression on his face, the Don continued more cheerfully, "But do not worry. Probably you won't know anything of all that. And you will get your schooling. Learn all you can. The Indians here will put your learning to good use."

Tomasito was quite unable to imagine why Don Joaquin should be so concerned about the Indians. Nothing seemed more in contrast to this elegant old mansion than the thatched huts of their mountain villages. But it was clear that for some reason Indians were the center of the man's life.

Don Joaquin was now hopping toward the door. "Come now, Don Pedro, let me show you my poor ruins. Yesterday's earthquake has really done for the old wing, I'm afraid. Cracked the whole north wall—down to the Inca foundation. Naturally, that is as solid as bedrock."

As he talked, he stepped briskly ahead of them along a corridor, then down a stairway into the courtyard. The west side of the patio was formed of a very old building of which the bottom third consisted of the familiar Inca masonry.

"Come around in back," invited Don Joaquin, opening a gate in the north wall. From the garden the damage to the old wing was evident as was the precarious condition of the roof; its tiles were scattered freely about on the ground.

"Not safe to go inside now, of course," commented Don Joaquin, "but you can see the extent of the area to be explored. We have never used the old wing except for storage. I haven't

33

even been in it for years. But my father used to keep his wine in the Inca cellar because of its thick stone walls. Must be rooms down there—maybe tombs. Think it's worth working on, Don Pedro?"

"By all means!" replied the archeologist. "Let me know when it is safe for us to start work. In the meantime, I'll study some of the old documents to see if there is any clue as to what kind of Inca building occupied this site."

Before Tomasito and Don Pedro took their leave, Don Joaquin shook his pointed finger at the boy. "Remember your great Indian heritage, my son," he admonished him. "Study hard and learn all you can in the United States. When you come back you will help to combine the social genius of the New World with the culture of the Old—to build a better Peru!"

"What did Don Joaquin mean?" Tomasito asked Don Pedro when they were in the car. "And why is he so much interested in the Indians? Isn't he a Spaniard?"

"Don Joaquin is not a Spaniard. He is a Peruvian. He has studied for many years the ways in which the villagers of Inca times worked together to grow their food, take care of the old and sick, provide fairly for every family, and maintain the Empire. He has been fighting in the national government for means by which to teach today's Indians these ancient arts so that they can have a better life and we can all have a stronger country. But the Incas, Tomasito, had no writing. So we would not know anything about them today, nor about any of the great ideas which have been important to the world, if it had not been for the books written by the Spaniards here, as well as those brought by them to this country from Europe. Don Joaquin means that we need the gifts of all people to make a great nation."

Tomasito's head throbbed with all the exciting new thoughts

which had entered it this morning. Don Pedro seemed to sense what the boy felt, for he drove silently, smiling occasionally, but adding no more words to the swirl of Tomasito's thoughts. Tomasito felt the affection of his friend and he no longer harbored ugly ideas about him. After all, they were all Peruvians!

When they reached the University they saw Jack and Teresa waiting for them at the entrance. Tomasito could tell at once that something was amiss. Jack, his hands in his pockets, was striding nervously back and forth, while Teresa looked anxiously up and down the streets and across the plaza.

"Ah, there you are, my brother!" she cried in relief as Tomasito ran toward her. "We must ask Don Pedro to excuse us," she continued, turning politely to the professor. "We cannot find Tío Dominguez. Jack thinks we should search for him on the road to Pisac. We must find him or the llamas will miss the train."

"Of course, *señora*," replied Don Pedro. "Just let me give two little gifts to my young student." From one of his coat pockets he extracted a rectangular brown-paper parcel, from another a small object wrapped like a mummy in soft cloth. "This," he said, holding out the brown package, "is a book—Cieza de Léon's account of his travels through Peru with the *Conquistadores*. When you read it, in California, you will see that he loved and admired the Incas almost as much as you do. Because he was such a careful student and thoughtful writer, he has left us a vivid picture of their life. When you are the age at which he wrote these notes, you will come back to me as fine a scholar as he!"

"And here," he continued, handing Tomasito the tiny cloth-wrapped bundle, "is the little clay llama. I think the cloth will keep it from breaking, but perhaps your sister will put it in her bag for safekeeping. As you look at it, remember our diggings!

35

May it inspire your mind to bear a harvest of ideas as rich as a field of Inca corn. God bless you, my son. I'll be waiting for you to come back. *Adiós, señora. Adiós,* Señor McGerraghty."

"Many, many thanks, Don Pedro!" cried Tomasito, almost in tears. *"Adiós, adiós!"*

The Llamas

"COME quickly, Tommy," urged Jack. "We are going to try to meet Tío Dominguez with a truck." Tomasito and Teresa had to run to keep up with Jack's long stride. They were out of breath by the time they reached the rented cattle truck parked a few blocks away.

Almost before Teresa had closed the cab door they set off, jouncing over the cobbled streets. As they climbed into the hilly northern section of the city the streets became so narrow that Tomasito gasped and Teresa shut her eyes, fearful that the wide truck would get stuck between the stone walls. During one nerve-shattering moment Jack had to back up a rock-lined lane in favor of an oncoming busload of tourists. At another point a detour became necessary because the street ended in a flight of steps down which a flock of sheep bumped and nudged their solemn way.

But at last they reached the open country outside the city and started upward along the mountain road. Even here, driving

37

was no task for the timid. The narrow winding road was occasionally frequented, always unexpectedly, by horseback riders, trucks, an occasional bus, and herds of sheep. There was evidence of yesterday's earthquake. Chunks of earth had fallen away from the edges of the road and Jack had to stop now and then to remove boulders from the path of the truck.

In spite of the hazards, Jack seemed to get a certain fierce satisfaction out of forcing the unwieldy truck up slippery grades and coaxing it around the crumbling edges of precipices. Now that they were out of the city, Tomasito and Teresa felt more at ease. They were used to harrowing mountain roads and the problems created by the frequent earthquakes.

But all three of them were beginning to worry seriously about Tío Dominguez. They had come almost a third of the way to Pisac, the sunlight was beginning to take on the slant of late afternoon, and still there was no sign of the old man and the llamas.

"I don't know if it's worth while going much farther," remarked Jack. "If we have to travel too far, we wouldn't get back to Cuzco by nightfall. I don't care to drive this road after dark in the condition it's in. And we wouldn't be able to make enough speed to catch the train anyway."

Teresa and Tomasito smiled and spoke to each other in Quechua. Teresa laughed shyly up at her husband.

"We thought you could make the truck spread its sides like wings and fly after dark like the owls," she teased. Jack grinned. He was pleased that his wife was impressed with his driving and, in turn, he was grateful that she and Tomasito were not timid and scary.

"I don't know what we'll do about the ship sailing," pondered Jack, "but we'll figure out something. We'll start back as soon as I can find a place to turn the truck around." They were now

38

rounding a huge shoulder of rock. As they came out on the other side, they saw that the road descended gently into a mountain valley before starting another steep ascent. At the base of the slope they could see a flat space to the right of the road, kept clear by the shade of giant eucalyptus trees. "Looks like a place to turn," remarked Jack.

But Tomasito and Teresa were peering into the dancing shadows under the big trees. "Llamas!" shouted Tomasito. "I think they are ours! See, there are four. Yes, there are Kuzni and Allca. Puca is over near the far tree and Quilla is lying down!"

"Are you sure? How can you tell so far away?" asked Jack. "I can hardly see that they're animals."

Tomasito and Teresa looked at him in surprise. Of course they could see them! Their eyes were used to great distances and they had learned to memorize the individual shapes of their animals from earliest childhood.

"What about Tío Dominguez?" inquired Jack.

"I can't see him yet," replied Teresa, "but he must be there. It is clear the llamas are listening to someone."

"Listening?"

"Oh, yes, now I see him," announced Teresa as the road bent a little to the left and approached the grove of trees. "See, he's playing his flute."

And now even Jack could see that she was right. Against the marbled trunk of the great tree, hidden from them until now, leaned a very old Indian in knee breeches and a tasseled poncho, his ancient, wrinkled face surmounted by the mushroom-like hat of Pisac. He was playing on an archaic clay flute. They could not yet hear the sound but it was clear the llamas could. Their ears were cocked, their solemn features as attentive and respectful as music lovers at a symphony.

"Probably he's waiting for Quilla to get up," observed Teresa.

"You know, Jack, there's no use trying to move a llama who wants to rest."

"*Díos mío!*" laughed Jack, letting the truck coast to a halt as quietly as possible so as not to frighten the enchanted group. The three silently climbed from the truck, but as soon as Teresa and Tomasito touched the ground the llamas moved their heads. Tío Dominguez was still absorbed in his music but the llamas had recognized their family. All of them looked at the young woman and the boy. Quilla stood up. Tomasito and Teresa ran to Tío Dominguez to greet him in Quechua, then patted and hugged each beloved animal.

After these greetings, Teresa talked to Tío Dominguez in Quechua, translating, with appropriately tactful modifications, the questions of her husband.

It turned out that Tío Dominguez had started from Pisac at the time agreed upon and had proceeded without incident until the earthquake. The quake had caused such a severe landslide that it had taken the old man hours to find a way over it.

Jack shook his head in amazement. He bowed to Tío Dominguez. "*Magnífico!*" he said, hoping that Tío Dominguez would understand from the Spanish his admiration and gratitude.

Jack turned to Teresa. "Ask him if he would like to ride to Cuzco with us and take the bus back?"

Teresa translated.

"Well, no thank you, *señor*," Tío Dominguez replied, looking somewhat dubiously at the truck. "I will walk slowly home after I have rested a little. There is a village a few miles back where I can spend the night."

Jack lowered the tailgate and Tomasito helped Teresa guide the llamas into the back of the truck.

"May I ride in the back, Señor Jack?" he asked.

40

"Yes, if you think the animals won't get panicky and trample you when we go around those bends," replied Jack.

"No, *señor*. I'll just tie this rope across the truck. They'll stay behind it." After tying the rope, Tomasito took his place between it and the cab of the truck. He talked soothingly to his friends as Jack fastened the tailgate, bowed to Tío Dominguez, and climbed into the cab.

The old Indian turned to Tomasito. "Good, my son!" he said solemnly. "I see you know how to talk to your animals. They need to be told about new things like trucks. Poor creatures! They will see many strange sights before they come to rest. It is good that you will be there to explain to them." The truck began to move. "Farewell, Tomasito. God be with you!" he cried.

As he waved to the old man, Tomasito thought with sadness that undoubtedly this would be the last time he would see the ancient and venerated head of his father's family.

The truck began to grind its way up the grade again and Tomasito had a hard time maintaining his balance. But it was good to be able to reach over and stroke Quilla's glistening white fur and to feel the coarse locks on Puca's long neck.

Standing up in the truck had its advantages for he could look out to see far over the valleys and gorges, while the wind tore at his hair and pushed the breath back in his throat. It was a glorious feeling. Allca was the only one of the llamas that seemed nervous. He did not attempt to move forward but he stamped, kicked, and tossed his head. Tomasito feared he might back up and kick at the tailgate. The boy managed to edge forward until he could put his arms around the frightened animal's neck, stroke his fur, and speak to him soothingly in Quechua. Soon the tall black and white creature began to quiet down and finally stood impassive like the others.

41

Night had fallen by the time they reached the outskirts of Cuzco. Soon they were passing through a small square in which a market fair had evidently taken place during the day. From a lighted building came the tempting aroma of cooking food. Jack stopped the truck, climbed out, and called to Tomasito. "You still here, Tommy? Are the llamas all right? I'm going to get us something to eat. Maybe you'd like to sit up in front with us now?"

Tomasito climbed into the cab with his sister. Teresa rubbed his cold hands and asked him about the llamas.

Jack soon returned, carrying skewers on which cubes of meat and peppers had been barbecued. Tomasito could not remember anything that had ever tasted so good. His stomach almost ached in gratitude.

"The train leaves at ten o'clock," said Jack, between bites. "It's eight now, so we don't have too much time to get across town and see that the animals are loaded. But it had been so long since we'd eaten I knew we couldn't wait till we got back from the station. Sure tastes good, doesn't it, Tommy?"

"*Sí, señor!*" replied Tomasito, with such depth of feeling that Jack and Teresa both laughed.

The truck started off again through the dark streets. Jack somehow managed to find his way around the crowded center of the city and to arrive at the railroad station a little after nine o'clock. He breathed a sigh of relief. Surely, with almost an hour to spare, it would be no problem to get the llamas into the cattle car in time.

Arrangements had already been made for the transportation of the animals. Jack had no trouble now in locating the freight office. However, when he finally came back to the truck after an attempt to find the freight master, he seemed a little uneasy.

"The men are all busy," he announced. "They have an extra

boxcar to load, then a flock of sheep to drive into the cattle car, before they load the llamas."

From the truck the three watched the freight men pushing dollies loaded with sacks and bales of hay.

"There's always something lonesome about a railroad station," observed Jack after a time. "Hear that whistle? It's the loneliest sound in the world. And the trains themselves, and the tracks always threading away into nowhere, leaving you behind—"

By the time the boxcar had been loaded, the clock in the station said nine-thirty. The men, not without difficulty, began to load the sheep into the railroad car.

Jack had been growing steadily more anxious and fidgety. "Let's get the llamas out of the truck, ready to go," he said to Tomasito. "It's only fifteen minutes before the train is due to start."

Jack let down the tailgate and Tomasito climbed in. For a minute or two he patted and stroked the llamas, talking to them softly. Then he coaxed Quilla to back down the ramp. He made a short hissing sound and the other three llamas turned and walked down the ramp as calmly as if they had been on the mountainside. At Tomasito's command, they stopped beside the truck and waited there with elegant sedateness.

The freight master and another railroad worker finally approached Jack. "I think we're ready now, *señor*. We two can drive the llamas into the car ourselves. The other men have gone to load another train."

"The boy can load them," Jack told him.

"Oh, no, *señor*," objected the man. "Only railroad employees are allowed on the freight platforms."

"Are you sure you can do it?" Jack asked anxiously.

"But of course, *señor!*" The freight master looked offended. "Only four animals?"

Jack and Tomasito glanced dubiously at each other. The two

43

railroad men got behind the animals, shouting at them in Spanish. The llamas made no move whatsoever. Almost without thinking, Tomasito gave a light whistle. The railroad men, who had paid no attention to the sound, looked somewhat shaken as the four llamas suddenly moved forward with long, swinging strides. Softly, Tomasito whistled again and, as abruptly as they had started, the animals stopped at the edge of the platform.

Now, however, the distance between the llamas and Tomasito made it impossible for him to communicate further with them. The trainmen would have to get them onto the car. But how?

The two men again shouted at the llamas who were standing stock-still. They slapped them on the haunches and even tried to push them up the ramp.

In this awkward fashion, they did manage, finally, to get Kuzni and Puca into the car. Now it was Allca's turn. The tall black and white beast looked scornfully down his nose at the impertinent strangers tugging at his neck fur and pushing on his haunches. Tomasito and Teresa, looking on in consternation, could almost feel him quiver with indignation.

"Jack, stop them!" cried Teresa. But before Jack could intervene, Allca had turned his head and had sent a long stream of saliva, mixed with chewed-up hay, hissing in the direction of the horrified freight master.

"*Díos mío!*" groaned Jack. "Tommy, come with me!" And, regulation or not, the two of them rushed to the side of the terrified and indignant beast. "Quick, Tommy, get him in!" commanded Jack.

While the freight master occupied himself with expressing his feelings and removing the llama's spittle, Tomasito patted and soothed the excited Allca. Finally, with one gentle whistle, he persuaded him to enter the car to join his brothers.

The freight master, evidently recognizing that regulations must go by the board, shouted from the sidelines and allowed Jack and Tomasito to take care of the llamas. The other railroad man seemed to find the situation amusing and grinned widely whenever his boss was not looking his way.

After settling Allca in the car Tomasito turned back for Quilla. He was not worried about her. The only female of the four, she was exceptionally gentle and docile. But just as he stepped onto the ramp he saw Quilla lie down! Heaven above! There she was, her pure-white fur gleaming like a queen's silks in the magic circle from an electric light. She was chewing her cud in immovable serenity. Tomasito knew that no amount of coaxing could move a llama who had decided to take a rest.

"Señor Jack!" he cried. "What shall we do? When Quilla lies down she just won't move till she's rested. I know her—I know she won't!"

"What!" cried Jack frantically. "You must try, Tomasito! See —the engine is getting ready to start. We can't leave her behind!"

Teresa, too, had grasped the situation. She and Tomasito knelt beside the resting llama. They coaxed and pleaded with her, knowing all the time that she would be deaf to their cries. Presently Teresa ceased beseeching and began praying to the Virgin. But heaven appeared to be on the side of Quilla, who continued to chew her cud imperturbably.

Jack paced back and forth, muttering to himself, "*Díos mío!* How in the world did I ever get myself tangled up with a bunch of crazy llamas!" There were shouts along the track and it was obvious the train would soon start. Suddenly Jack stopped.

"No goose-necked llama is going to make a monkey out of

45

me!" he shouted. He strode over to a nearby dolly and sent it spinning in the direction of Tomasito and Quilla. "Come, Tommy—and you, too." He beckoned to the railroad man. Then he clasped Quilla around her hind quarters. The railroad man picked her up in front and before the stupefied llama had time to spit they had dumped her onto the dolly and had wheeled her up the ramp. They deposited her on the straw-covered floor of the boxcar. Tomasito had time to speak but a few words of comfort to her before the ramp was removed, the door closed, and the signal given for the train to start.

"Whew!" breathed Jack, wiping his forehead with his sleeve. He handed the railroad men some coins and solemnly thanked them for their efforts.

When they were at last back in the truck Jack said to Tomasito, "My boy, I've seen stubborn mules, and even a pigheaded camel or two, but those llamas are the orneriest animals on earth!"

"Oh, no, *señor!*" protested Tomasito. "Llamas are lovely, gentle creatures. But they are proud—and besides, they only know Quechua."

Tomasito was shocked at himself for having dared to contradict a grown man but Jack only laughed.

"Well, I'm sure glad they load them on the ship with a crane!" he said with a chuckle.

46

At Sea

TOMASITO stood at the ship's rail, looking out over the gray and green ridges of the morning sea. For the first time in his life he could not see his homeland. And yet, for the first time in days, he felt close to the mountains. As far as the eye could see, the expanse of swells and troughs, mountains and valleys of water, was not dissimilar to the distant ranges of the Andes.

Here there were creatures different from the ones at home, and yet understandable to him. The silvery gulls, swooping and wheeling around the ship, knew how to ride the wind like the hawks and condors of the mountains. A school of dolphins was keeping the ship company and Tomasito watched in delighted fascination as they played and danced, as if to show the passengers what perfect joy it was to live in water. Tomasito had never seen any animals like these and yet their rhythmic grace somehow reminded him of his llamas swaying along the mountain trails, as perfectly at home in the thin air and chilly fogs of their own special place as the dolphins were in theirs.

47

The ship, so strangely metallic and geometrical, full of curious instruments and weird sounds, a short time ago would have filled him with awe. But he had seen so much within the past few days that there was no more room for wonder in his mind.

The day after they had shipped the llamas from Cuzco, Jack and Teresa and Tomasito had boarded a plane for Lima. Tomasito had been filled with amazement as they approached the huge metal bird. But somehow the flight itself had disappointed him. There was nothing like the exhilarating motion and breathtaking struggle with the wind which had so thrilled him during the truck ride on the mountain. Here in the plane the cramped confinement of the cabin, the steady drone of the engines, and their imperceptible progress through the air made it hard to believe that they were in flight through the sky.

Lima, the brilliant capital of his country, remained in his memory as a blur of flowers, fountains, ornate palaces, and, most of all, wheels—wheels of all kinds. Bicycle wheels, shiny silver discs on sleek limousines, huge truck wheels, taller than Tomasito himself—all in motion, rolling, spinning in a dizzying stream. He had felt uprooted, like a plant torn loose from a canyon wall and carried along by a mountain torrent. Nowhere did he see a familiar sight. Thousands and thousands of strange people dressed in stiff clothing moved like an army of mechanical dolls through the streets. The familiar sounds of wind and rushing water had been displaced by the strident squawking of horns and the perpetual roar of the great procession of wheels.

Tomasito had followed docilely behind Jack and Teresa as they walked through the endless corridors of famous buildings. He sat behind them in the buses that rolled them past an endless succession of fountained squares. More and more he felt alone. There was room for only two on a bus seat. Jack and

48

Teresa sat together and he sat behind them, sometimes with one of the doll-like strangers.

Teresa was enchanted with the capital. She gazed in rapture at the gilded statues and stood transfixed before the store windows filled with elegant garments and glittering jewels. Jack was happy to be her guide through so much splendor. He took her into one of the fine shops and bought her city clothes. Back at the hotel she tried on her new finery. Jack was very proud and even Tomasito had to admit that she looked as elegant as any Lima lady. But the wool dress with its narrow skirt, the shoes with thin spike heels, her hair drawn up on top of her head, made her look so unlike the Teresa who had climbed in her bare feet up the cobbled slopes of the ruins that Tomasito felt he had lost his sister.

"Let us send post cards to Papá," said Teresa one afternoon. So they selected some from the shop in the hotel lobby and wrote Papá's name and address on them. As Tomasito thought of the cards flying back to the mountains and traveling on the yellow car, he was overcome with such a yearning to go with them that he could not write. Teresa finally wrote something for him, then said, "Go now, Tomasito. Run down to the post box on the corner and mail these. Papá will be waiting to hear from us."

Tomasito had pushed his way out the hotel door and into the stream of strangers. He had moved blindly, as if carried along by the crowd, to the corner mailbox. He stood there, holding the cards. In his mind he could see Papá coming home to their stone house, the cards in his hand. He could see Domitila and Rosita and Jacinto reaching for them, and he could see the distant, lonely look in his father's eyes.

Somehow he had not been able to let go of the cards. He held them stiffly between thumb and fingers and moved on

49

along the street—unseeing, drifting with the stream of people. He was so stupefied by his homesickness that he no longer saw the world around him. He walked and walked the endless streets, paying no attention to where he was or to the passage of time.

Dusk was beginning to fall and suddenly the street lights flared up along the avenue on which Tomasito had been walking. He was startled. Gradually he became aware of his surroundings, the strange street and the unknown square. As his eyes began to look outward, they focused on a familiar shape standing on a stone block—the figure of a llama. His mind was still crowded with the images of his home and for a moment it was hard for him to tell what was real. But as he moved toward the animal he could see that it was made of bronze. It was the famous llama statue which they had glimpsed from a sightseeing bus. The familiar shape, sharp against the evening sky, brought him back to the present.

"No, my father," he thought to himself. "I won't disappoint you. I couldn't run away from our llamas." And then he remembered that by tomorrow the nightmare of the big city would be over and he would be on the ship with his beloved animals.

He had found a policeman then and was put on a bus that went past the hotel. Teresa and Jack had been frantic, of course. Jack roared at him and even swore, which somehow made him feel better, and Teresa clasped him in her arms, talking to him in Quechua.

"Where were you, my brother?" she cried.

"I saw the llama," he said, not knowing how to explain. But Teresa had understood.

"Ay, Tomasito," she said, with tears in her eyes, "The mountains seem so far away. But you must come with me. I need you —to take care of the llamas and to talk to me of home!"

"The Captain wants to know if you would like to see your llamas?" Tomasito, leaning against the ship's rail, was suddenly aware that Jack had appeared beside him. With him was a tall, thin man in a blue uniform.

"But *sí!*" cried Tomasito.

The tall man smiled and said something in a strange language to a seaman nearby.

"Come on," said Jack in Spanish. "The sailor will show us the way to the hold."

The sailor held open a heavy metal door, they descended slippery metal ladders, and followed several passageways down into the dark center of the ship. Tomasito, who had learned to keep his balance on the slick stone stairways of Inca terraces, felt the curious motion of the ship—a rocking not unlike that of an earthquake, but steady and unending. He began to be aware of his stomach.

After a series of tunnels, which Tomasito thought would surely bring them to the bottom of the sea, they entered a spacious compartment which was divided into rows of stalls. The boy's nose welcomed the familiar smell of animals.

At first the only animals he could see were cattle, most of them lying placidly in straw-filled cubicles. But as his eyes eagerly searched the stalls, he caught sight of black and white haunches, dripping with fur, and a stubby tail—unmistakably a llama!

"Allca!" shouted Tomasito. He flew down the aisle, bolted the barrier, and clasped his arms around Allca's neck. Since the llamas were so small, two of them had been housed in one stall and presently he found himself hugging Kuzni too. And, to his joy, there were Puca and Quilla right next door!

To the seamen and Jack, who looked on with a grin, the reunion seemed a pretty one-sided affair. Tomasito petted and

51

stroked his cherished animals, talking away to them in Quechua, while the llamas, dignified and aloof as ever, silently chewed hay. But Tomasito knew better. The gentle nudges and bumps he received as he squeezed between them, the alert tension of their ears, made him know that they recognized and understood him and were welcoming him in their own way.

"The Captain says you may come to see your llamas whenever you wish," announced Jack as they began to work their way back again to the deck. "Just be sure, though, that you remember your way and don't get lost."

"Let me show you," replied Tomasito. "I'll go ahead and lead you back." Without a moment's hesitation, he conducted the two men through the passageways, up the ladders, around corners, through more passageways, up more ladders, until there they were once more back on the deck where they had started.

The men exchanged exclamations.

"Tommy, how'd you do it?" asked Jack admiringly. "And without even a compass!"

"We don't use compasses in the mountains, Señor Jack." That was all Tomasito said in explanation but he smiled shyly. "Don't worry, *señor*. I can find my llamas."

On their way up from the hold Tomasito had noticed that the rocking motion of the ship had become more pronounced. It was hard to open the door onto the deck because of the force of the wind which was stirring the waves into foamy green piles and tossing spray onto the deck.

Tomasito was astonished by the roughness of the waves whose earlier serenity had reminded him of the mountain ridges of the Andes. Now it was as if the raging Urubamba River had suddenly risen in a gigantic flood and had poured itself in tumult over the scenery. He clung to the rail along the cabin wall and tried to accustom himself to the increasing rolling and thrashing of the ship.

The storm continued to increase in violence throughout the day. The few passengers on the freighter retired to their cabins in distress, with the exception of Jack, who had found the "sea legs" developed during his years in the Navy, and Tomasito who resolutely suppressed any inclination to be sick because he was afraid he would miss some of the excitement of the storm.

Jack did his best to comfort Teresa, who was miserably ill as well as frightened by the howling wind, the crashing water, and the shuddering vessel. Shortly after dinner he made sure that Tomasito was safely installed in his bunk, then returned to help poor Teresa as much as he could.

In the morning the storm, though somewhat diminished in intensity, still shook the feeble vessel like an incessant earthquake. Jack, aroused by the growing light of dawn, began to wonder if his young brother-in-law had maintained his courage throughout the turmoil of the night.

When he found Tomasito's bunk empty, he smiled to himself. "That's a kid for you. Probably down below giving the cook a workout."

But Jack found that Tomasito was not at breakfast. None of the ship's officers, who were alone at the breakfast table, had seen him. The boy was not in the lounge, either, and the deck, still awash, was empty. Jack began to be thoroughly alarmed. Could the mountain boy have tried to go out on deck?

The Captain, informed of the missing boy, began a survey of his crew. One of the first men he questioned was the seaman who had been Tomasito's guide the day before. "Did you look in the hold, sir?" the man asked. "He might have been worried about his llamas."

53

"But how could he have found his way below in a storm like this one?"

"That boy, sir, could find his way to his llamas at the bottom of the sea!" the sailor answered.

"The man may be right, sir," agreed Jack. "I wouldn't put it past him. Let's look."

As they entered the hold, Tomasito was nowhere in sight. Jack looked closely into the shadowed llama stalls. The llamas were lying down, calmly rolling back and forth with the motion of the ship. At the far end of Allca's pen Jack caught sight of something white. It was Tomasito's shirt. The boy lay sound asleep in the straw, his fingers clinging firmly to the woolen tassels on Allca's neck.

"That llama's the excitable one," explained Jack. "Tommy must have been afraid Allca would get panicky in the storm. He may have saved the poor creature's life by coming here!"

Later, Tomasito was astonished that Jack had been anxious. "But you told me, Señor Jack," he protested, "that the Captain said I could come to my llamas whenever I liked!"

Harvest

BY AND large, Tomasito found life on the freighter not at all unpleasant. Now that the storm was over, he watched the sea for hours, fascinated by the constantly changing landscape of watery mountain ranges. And he had the llamas for company. Every day he found his way through the maze of the ship to visit his friends. He talked to them, walked them up and down between the rows of stalls, and played to them on his clay flute the ancient tunes of their homeland. Thus the great change in their environment was made easier for the animals. Actually, they seemed to wait as patiently on the tilting ship as on the slopes of the Andes.

The ship itself was filled with interest. Since there were few passengers, the ship's officers soon became acquainted with all the travelers. They took special interest in the young Peruvian who was making the acquaintance of the sea for the first time. Sometimes the Captain would show him special wonders—the powerful engines throbbing away in the depths of the ship, the radio, the compass, and other magic devices.

But it seemed harder to converse with people than with the animals. Tomasito understood what the llamas were trying to say to him and they in turn listened contentedly, whether he spoke in Spanish or in Quechua or merely played to them on his flute. He could tell that the ship's officers were friendly and he marveled at the sights they showed him. But even when they spoke in Spanish, he could not comprehend explanations of the curious objects surrounding him. Sometimes Jack would try to help. But how could he describe to a young boy who had spent his life herding llamas on an Andean mountain peak the intricate mechanics of radar?

In fact, Jack was hard put to fulfill his duties as a teacher. He had imagined that on the slow freighter voyage to North America Tomasito and Teresa would somehow absorb enough English to get them started in that language. He himself had managed to pick up Spanish. But he had long since forgotten his struggles and the many months and years it had taken him to be able to change freely from one language to the other.

Things weren't turning out exactly as he had hoped. Teresa, even after the storm had subsided, continued to be miserably seasick. Jack was awkward and impatient when he tried to pin Tomasito down to the lessons which neither he nor the boy felt comfortable about. Finally, Jack gave up and lessons were no longer mentioned. He divided his time between trying to comfort Teresa and exchanging yarns with the crew and the other passengers.

It was fortunate that Tomasito was accustomed to solitude and to the company of animals for he had become almost mute in the presence of human beings. No one could speak Quechua except Teresa, with whom he exchanged a few words only at

56

bedtime. The people who talked Spanish spoke thoughts he could not understand. The English which flowed so exuberantly from Jack's lips as he sat with the Captain over their evening beer made no more sense to him than the rumblings of the Lima traffic.

Even more painful, at the dinner table each evening Jack and the other adults would start out by calling the boy's attention to various objects, giving them their English names.

"Salt!" somebody would say loudly, thumping the heavy salt cellar down before him. Or, "Spoon, Tommy!" And a spoon would be waved rudely in his face. There seemed to be a feeling among these volunteer teachers that he spoke no English because he was deaf, or perhaps had difficulty in seeing the objects named. If Tomasito hesitated in repeating the name of an object, the adult would shout it more loudly still.

Before each meal, the thought of sitting helpless while six or eight grownups fixed their eyes on him and took turns shouting at him was almost more than he could bear. If he had not been always so hungry he would have skipped mealtime altogether and tried to hide. But then Jack would have noticed and there would have been another big fuss as on the day of the storm. Fortunately, although the grownups continued to pounce upon him with their English words as soon as he appeared at the table, they eventually grew tired of this game and forgot about him before the meal was over.

As far as Tomasito knew, he was the only child on the ship. One evening he slid as unobtrusively as possible into his place at the table. As he looked up timidily from his plate, much to his surprise he saw a new face next to the Captain. It was a girl's face, gentle and shy. She had blue eyes and her hair, braided in two plaits, looked like palest silk.

"My daughter Margit," announced the Captain. This much

57

Tomasito understood. "This is her first trip with me. It is the first time she has felt like coming to the table."

The passengers began at once to greet the little girl and to ask her silly questions, in the manner of adults. The child turned her head away and finally hid it against her father's shoulder.

The Captain made some explanation to the passengers which Tomasito did not follow. Later, Jack told him that the girl knew only Norwegian, though the Captain spoke several languages. The passengers had wanted to begin at once to teach her English but her father had explained that she still didn't feel too well. "Girls are lucky!" Tomasito thought.

Much as Tomasito hated his "English lessons," he began to worry about the days ahead. Slowly, he was beginning to realize that in Jack's country everybody would speak English! Jack's neighbors, the boys he might want to play with, the people who would come to ride the llamas—all would speak English. The teacher would talk English in the school!

The last thought filled him with panic. Suppose he could not understand the teacher? How would he learn the history and mathematics and science he would need in order to become Don Pedro's assistant?

To avoid these gloomy, unwelcome fantasies, Tomasito's mind turned to the past, to his happy visit with Don Pedro in Cuzco, and, finally, to the presents his friend had given him.

"I must look at the little clay llama," he thought. "Perhaps it will help me to grow a crop of English words."

Tomasito knocked on Teresa's cabin door. She was sitting up in her bunk, looking thin and pale, but not quite so greenish as she had on other days. She held out her arms to him and said in lovely, clicking Quechua, "Ah, my brother, come to me. How I have missed you! Come, tell me about the llamas and about everything you have done while I have been ill."

58

In answer, Quechua words poured like a mountain stream from Tomasito's lips. He felt as though his thoughts had suddenly thawed.

Presently, he told her of his trouble with English. "What will I do, my sister, if I cannot understand the teachers?" he cried.

"You will learn," she assured him. "Don't you remember? We didn't know Spanish when we first went to school. But it grew in our minds before we knew it!"

That was right, Tomasito agreed. He had learned Spanish without really thinking about it. But he was certainly thinking about English! Still, he didn't feel confident.

"I have come for the little clay llama," he told his sister. "Don Pedro said it might help my thoughts to grow like the corn in the Inca fields." Teresa laughed as she took the little object, wrapped so carefully in its rags, from her handbag. Tomasito carefully unwound the strips of cloth and gazed fondly at the little clay animal lying in the palm of his hand.

"Grow me new English words," he said silently to the llama. So firmly did he believe in Inca magic that he half expected to see words on paper banners unroll from the llama's lips, as they seemed to do in pictures he had seen in Don Pedro's ancient books.

"Perhaps the English words will come tomorrow," he pretended as he nested the little relic in a pocket of his suitcase.

The next day, when he thought the deck was deserted, Tomasito took his clay flute to the ship's rail and began to play softly to himself. Suddenly he had an eerie sensation. He played a simple phrase. Above the sound of the wind and water he heard the same ancient melody repeated, exactly as he had played it. He tried another phrase. Again it was repeated. His scalp began to prickle. He remembered the tales Tío Dominguez had told him about the spirits. He turned his head ever so cautiously. As he did so, a stab of light caught his eye. A few yards further along the rail stood the other flutist. The flute, a long thin tube of gleaming silver, was being fingered by the Captain's daughter.

This time, the girl did not appear so pale and shy. Her cheeks were pink from the wind and her blue eyes, full of mischief, laughed at him. Tomasito laughed back. Then he played a tune. Margit played it after him. Then she played a tune of her own. Tomasito copied it. They went on imitating each other for some time, until they found that while Margit could play almost the same sounds as Tomasito, the boy could not always copy Margit. They examined and compared the two flutes.

"*Más agujeros*," exclaimed Tomasito, running his finger along the silver flute.

"*Mere hüller*," said Margit, almost at the same moment.

The two children looked at each other in surprise. Margit had been speaking in Norwegian, Tomasito in Spanish, but they knew they had both said the same thing—just like the two flutes playing the same melody!

"*Hülle!*" said Margit, pointing to a hole in the flute. She made her face look very serious and shouted the word as if Tomasito were deaf.

"*Agujero!*" shouted Tomasito back, looking just as stern.

As they burst into laughter, a voice near them shouted "*Hole!*" It was Jack. They all laughed together then, and the children went on playing the new game, imitating the passengers so realistically that Jack began to look around to make sure that none of them were listening.

At the dinner table that night, Margit and Tomasito were quiet and solemn but they dared not look at each other. They repeated the words shouted at them very meekly. When the grownups finally began to talk among themselves, Margit made a face at Tomasito. Even Jack winked at the children. Tomasito, remembering his manners, looked down at his plate.

Every day after that Margit and Tomasito played the word game, hiding on some part of the deck so that they could make fun of their tormentors. They devised all sorts of ways of catching each other up. Tomasito would ask Jack to teach him words for objects which Margit couldn't name and Margit would try to pick up from her father whole sentences in English in order to impress Tomasito.

One day Jack informed Tomasito that Margit had gotten permission from the Captain to go with him to see the llamas. Tomasito was delighted. He went first to his cabin to get his Inca flute. As he looked in his suitcase, he glanced at the little llama wrapped in its cloth.

"I must show her this, too," he thought, and stuffed it into his pocket.

Margit was enchanted with the four llamas. She petted them, called them by name, and watched them at they listened to Tomasito's music. Suddenly she remembered their game.

"Llama," she said, pointing to Kuzni.

"Sí, llama," affirmed Tomasito.

Tomasito remembered the Inca relic and pulled it from his pocket.

"Inca llama," he announced, unwrapping it carefully. Margit stroked the tiny object with her finger. She nodded her head in understanding.

"Inca llama," she agreed.

As Tomasito looked at the little clay llama, which his ancestors had thought brought bountiful harvests to their fields, he thought, "Why, the magic has begun to work. The English words are already sprouting in my mind!"

61

The Golden Gate

THE long voyage which, to Tomasito and certainly to Teresa, had begun to seem interminable, finally was about to end.

"Tomorrow we will be in San Francisco!" announced Jack. Tomasito was so excited that he could scarcely sleep. The next morning he rushed out on deck and propped himself against the landward rail. Teresa had recovered sufficiently to muster the strength to busy herself with packing and to concern herself with her own and her brother's appearance. It was almost impossible to dislodge Tomasito from the ship's rail, but she eventually persuaded him to dress himself in a manner suitable to his entrance into a new world.

"Will we herd the llamas to your home, Señor Jack?" asked Tomasito as Jack stood beside him at the rail.

"We'll use a truck, Tommy. San Francisco is like Lima. It is far from the mountains. I'll rent a truck and we'll all go to-gether."

"Tonight?"

"No, I don't think I'd like to drive all night. We'll leave tomorrow. Besides, I'd like to talk to the zoo director in the morning and get some ideas about taking care of llamas in California."

"The San Francisco Zoo?" inquired Tomasito. He felt uneasy. Images from his dream about the zoo and the Golden Enclosure crossed his mind. But there was no time to ask further questions. The shore, before now a long gray streak on the eastern horizon, began to take on detail.

"We're almost there, Tommy!" Tomasito could tell that Jack was excited too. "I'm going to get Teresa."

Tomasito knew by the bustle on deck, the sounds of moving cables, hatches opening and closing, orders being shouted, that the harbor was near. "The llamas!" he thought. "I must tell them we have arrived."

He made his way down to the hold cautiously, not wanting to get in the way of the crew. Luckily, it was still possible for him to reach the animals. He put his arms around them, caressed them, and told them in Quechua about the new adventure.

"Soon you will be in the light and air," he explained. "Do not fear when they lift you up high. You will come down safely. And we will soon come to take you to the mountains. Think of it, Allca! Soon you will walk free again on a mountain!"

Back on deck, he saw Margit waving to him from the bridge.

"Papa say, stay here," she called. "Good-by, Tomasito!"

"*Adiós!*" he called back.

"Say good-by llamas!" called Margit again.

"Come see llamas, Parson's Flat," Tomasito tried to explain. "*Adiós,* Margit!"

The afternoon passed slowly for Tomasito at his post by the rail. Presently he was joined by Jack and Teresa. Jack began to comment on the islands they were passing and pointed ahead to a bridge in the distance. "The Golden Gate!" he announced.

As the freighter moved in closer, the bridge ahead looked more and more like a golden gate, its towers now burnished by the evening sun. The headlands to the right and the hills beyond glittered in the sunset as though set with jewels. The freighter was now moving under the immense bridge. Tomasito and Teresa gazed, mute and motionless, at the sight of the dazzling city skyline. Jack seemed to sense their bewilderment and put his arms around their shoulders. "Don't worry, kids. I'll not let you get lost!"

The morning after their arrival in San Francisco (they had spent the night in a downtown hotel), Jack announced that they had two chores to attend to before setting off for Parson's Flat. One was to buy Tomasito some clothes suitable for wear in his new home. The other was to consult the zoo officials concerning the care of the llamas in California. Teresa was eager to look in the shop windows and to see the sights of her new land. But Tomasito wasn't interested in the big city with its noisy crowds and longed to get into the truck and start for the mountains.

"Let's go in here!" said Jack, turning into a huge store on Market Street. When they reached the "Boy's Department" Tomasito's stoic endurance of a tiresome necessity suddenly turned into delight.

"How'd you like an outfit like that, Tommy?" asked Jack, pointing to one of the dummies dressed in blue jeans, a plaid shirt, denim stock jacket, and a broad-brimmed hat, just like the cowboys Tomasito had admired in movies shown on shipboard.

"For me?" he asked in such surprise that Jack and Teresa had to laugh.

"Of course," replied Jack. "That's what boys wear in the mountains. After all, you'll be a stockman, taking care of those llamas."

64

Tomasito was speechless as the clerk fitted him with the completely new outfit.

"You'd better wait to wear the hat," suggested Jack. "This San Francisco wind'd blow it into the bay. And I think we'll wait to get the boots till we get over in the valley."

"*Ay,* my brother!" exclaimed Teresa. "You look just like a cowboy!"

Tomasito looked at himself in the long mirror and was indeed impressed. He smiled at his brown face under the jaunty hat. His legs could be longer, he thought, but he was still pleased with his new appearance. He happily clutched the big package of "extras" which the clerk handed him and, wearing his crisp new denims, he strolled with Jack and Teresa through the city streets to the streetcar that would take them to the zoo.

At the zoo there was no time to stop and look at animals. "We must get to the zoo keeper's office by eleven," Jack reminded them. They passed a sign that pointed ahead, "To the Llamas." Even Tomasito could read it. He started. It was like his dream! He remembered that Tío Dominguez thought the spirits could show you the future in your sleep.

He dared not run away and trotted along behind Jack until they came to the llama pen. Tomasito sighed with relief. No golden llamas—just ordinary brown-and-white ones, munching away with dignity. There were not many of them, however, and no babies.

"They are supposed to be hard to raise at low altitudes, I think," said Jack.

The zoo director was on vacation, but an assistant, Mr. Hansen, received them. Tomasito tried hard to follow the conversation but he could tell that the English words and phrases he had learned on the ship were pathetically insufficient for the pur-

65

pose. Finally Jack noticed the dismay on Tomasito's face and began to translate some of the zoo keeper's remarks.

"Mr. Hansen thinks we'll have to buy hay for the llamas in the winter, Tommy. They can stand the cold in the Sierras all right, but the snow will keep them from getting enough fodder."

As the men talked, Tomasito kept his eyes fixed on their faces. Jack shook his head several times as if in doubt. "Mr. Hansen wants us to sell him Quilla," Jack interpreted. "He says the zoo needs a female and he will give us a good price for her. You know we cannot use a female for the rides."

Tomasito felt hollow inside, drained of all feeling. He had been taught never to contradict or argue with grownups, but he soon found himself pleading with Jack.

"Please, please, Señor Jack! Don't sell Quilla. She has been with me and Teresa and Kuzni and Puca and Allca all her life. She would be so sad here in the zoo. How could we get along without her?"

"I know you'd hate to part with her, Tommy, but if the llamas can't graze during the winter they might eat up all the money we made on the summer rides."

Tomasito had never heard of selling a member of the family because you couldn't make money on her. To him the llamas were part of his family. But he could see that this was important to Jack. "Perhaps that's why all those North Americans are rich!" he thought bitterly. Then he remembered that Papá too had wanted him to take care of the llamas to make money to pay for his own food.

"Señor Jack, I will gather hay for the winter myself," he pleaded. "And Teresa will help, won't you, Teresa?" Teresa looked almost as anxious as her brother.

"Oh, yes, brother! Please, Jack!" she implored.

"But you two just don't know how impossible that would be," insisted Jack. "By the time you found out you couldn't do it, it would be too late to sell Quilla. This is a good deal." Mr. Hansen, seeing the sadness in their eyes, said something reassuring to Jack.

"Mr. Hansen says you could come and visit Quilla whenever you wished," reported Jack.

But Tomasito and Teresa were not to be comforted. How would they get to San Francisco "whenever they wanted"? And would they want to visit Quilla? It would be like going to see her in prison!

"Señor Jack," objected Tomasito as respectfully as he could. "Papá thought Allca might become ugly without a female around. He might spit at the children. That was one reason he sent Quilla with the others."

Jack looked thoughtful. After questioning Mr. Hansen, he said, "'Perhaps you have a point there, Tommy. Mr. Hansen says it could happen. These llamas are getting to look like more trouble than I thought. Maybe I should sell them all to the zoo!"

Tomasito and Teresa were stunned. Tomasito felt hatred for Jack and for everything North American surging through him. He would run away and stow away on a ship going back to Peru. But then he looked across at Teresa. How could he leave her with this heartless stranger!

Jack had begun again to talk to Mr. Hansen. Suddenly Tomasito touched his sleeve. "Señor Jack," he proposed hesitatingly, "we will need a female to replace our herd. But we could also raise llamas for the zoo. It might be easier in the high altitudes. Please let us keep Quilla. Then we could send her first kid to Mr. Hansen. Perhaps we could even raise some for other zoos."

"Oh!" groaned Jack. "We not only have to contend with spitting llamas and no fodder, but you want to raise them! It

67

may be crazy, but who says only the Yankees have ingenuity?" He thought a moment and then repeated Tomasito's proposal to Mr. Hansen in English. The man smiled and put his hand on Tomasito's shoulder admiringly.

"That might not be a bad idea," translated Jack. "In fact, he says we might make more money raising lllamas for zoos than we would with the llama rides!"

Jack held out his hand to Tomasito. "You win, boy! Now just be sure you can raise those kids!"

Tomasito and Teresa broke into broad smiles.

"*Gracias! Gracias!*" Teresa cried.

And Tomasito said proudly, "I will work hard, Señor Jack." Then he turned to Mr. Hansen. "Thank you very much. I bring llama," he said in his best English.

As Tomasito went past the sign pointing to the llamas, he thought, "It is true. I *did* save my llamas. I did it myself. And I will not let these Yankees turn them to gold!"

Mountains Again

TOMASITO felt himself beginning to wake up. There was a crook in his neck. The edge of the shoe box containing the new boots Jack had bought him in Stockton cut into the back of his head. The straw in the bed of the truck pricked through his shirt. Just then he felt himself tilted at an angle as the truck climbed an incline. They were in the foothills.

He was suddenly very wide awake. As he stood up, he could see the black ribbon of the road behind him. In the distance it ran straight and flat through the shimmering heat waves of the valley floor. He worked his way past the llamas to look out the side of the truck. The hills immediately ahead were dark green. Soon they would be climbing through thick forests. As the truck reached the top of the incline, it turned sharply to the right and began to circle the hill. Suddenly they were on a bluff high above a canyon. Tomasito gasped. Ahead rose ridge after ridge of blue mountains. Above them were mountain peaks glistening with patches of snow!

"The mountains, Allca, the mountains!" Tomasito almost sobbed. He pulled Allca's head over to the side of the truck to show him the glorious sight.

The mountain road was smooth and the truck climbed with a steady drone of its engine. The wind began to whistle past Tomasito's ears as he stood in the truck bed, and whenever the road followed a canyon rim he felt once more as if he were gliding along on air currents, like the hawks and eagles which circled above them.

Tomasito and Teresa had never seen such forests. Jack drove them through the grove of giant redwoods at Calaveras in order to show off one of the wonders of California. The two Peruvians stared and said "Ay!" at the sight of the huge trees. But they were eager to go on.

As the day wore on, the forests became more sparse. Now they were in a region of huge gray boulders. There were pines and cedars spaced among the masses of rock and wiry bushes with small dark leaves. Up here, in the middle of June, it was still spring. There were patches of snow on sheltered slopes. Wildflowers of burning scarlet and electric blue illumined the little meadows and the ledges between the rocks. The direct rays of the sun were searing, but the air had grown thin and cutting and when they passed into the shade of a rock wall the cold wind stabbed insolently at Tomasito. The boy felt charged, as if the sun and biting air were sending competing currents through his body. The llamas too were tense. Their ears pricked forward, stiff and sharp.

They came finally to a meadow of considerable size with a tiny stream running through it. A thick coat of new grasses softened the rocky ground between larger boulders. Jack parked the truck. "We're at the top of the pass, Tommy!" he

70

called to the boy. "Come and see the view. We'll give the llamas a treat too!"

He lowered the tailgate and Tomasito gave the llamas the ancient signals to move. They turned slowly and descended with dignity into the fragrant meadow.

"Let them graze awhile, Tommy," Jack said. "We'll have a drink from the stream and a snack ourselves. But first let me show you something." He took Teresa's hand and led her and the boy to a table of rock in the center of the meadow. Teresa laughed and kicked off her shoes. Soon Tomasito was barefoot too. Their toes felt for the familiar roughness of the rock as they ran deftly up its steep side. At the top they looked to the east and their faces became still with awe.

"*Our* mountains!" Tomasito breathed.

Ridge after ridge of snow-covered mountains seemed to enclose the horizon. Tomasito suddenly began to feel sheltered and safe. For the first time, he had hope that California could become a home.

Jack was hungry and he brought out the sandwiches they had picked up in Stockton. But Tomasito and Teresa, seated on the great rock, could hardly be distracted from the view.

"We are just about as high here as your ruins in Peru," Jack told them. "Nine thousand feet."

"If only the earth were as straight as it looks on the map, we could look south and wave to Papá from our peak to his," thought Tomasito.

At last Jack said they must be on their way. "Sit with us, Tommy," he suggested when the llamas were safely back in the truck. "You can see better from the cab." Thankfully, Tomasito climbed in between Jack and Teresa. This was the last lap of the journey to Parson's Flat, their new home, and sister and brother needed each other.

71

The road passed for a short distance through flat grasslands, then plunged downward, hugging the sheer rock wall and skirting the edges of space.

"How high is Parson's Flat?" asked Tomasito presently.

"About six thousand feet," answered Jack. "It's in a meadowland between two passes. We were quite isolated up here when I was a boy, but now a good highway goes from Parson's Flat to Lake Tahoe. Cabins are being built along the river and on the nearby lakes. Parson's Flat has lots of summer visitors. In fact, my brother says they now have tourists even in the winter. There's pretty good skiing on some of the slopes."

The road had now left the rock wall and was descending into the flatland. It was early evening and the valley was in deep shadow. The sky was still luminous and the mountain peaks to the east burned with reflected sunset.

A little later, Jack turned on his headlights. Suddenly he exclaimed, "There it is, kids! There's Parson's Flat. It won't be long now!" He gestured toward a string of lights in the distance and pressed down on the accelerator. Tomasito and Teresa were silent and Teresa reached over and touched her brother's hand.

Lighted windows began to appear through the trees along the road. At last they came to a cluster of buildings—a gas station, a store, and several restaurants with blinking signs. "The main street of Parson's Flat," Jack announced happily. "Well, the sheriff's office is still the same, I see, and old Sorenson still has his store. I wonder what all those sheds are. They look like government buildings." He slowed the truck to a crawl now, searching for familiar landmarks.

As they left the main street Jack said, "Look for the Sierra Motel, Tommy, on the left. We're just about a mile beyond that. There it is!"

A lighted sign said "Sierra Motel" and beyond it the lights of two houses appeared through pine trees. In the glare from the headlights they could see two mail boxes, each labelled "Mc-Gerraghty." Jack turned the truck abruptly into a driveway, pounding sharply on the horn as he did so.

Before the truck had come to a halt Tomasito saw the door of the nearest house open and a young boy, followed by a man and woman, come racing toward the driveway. Jack leaped from the truck to greet his brother's family.

"Come, Teresa and Tommy!" he called presently, after the first salutations were over. He opened the door of the truck and lifted Teresa to the ground. Despite his nervousness, Tomasito managed to follow.

"This is your Aunt Kathy and Uncle Pat," Jack was saying. Tomasito shyly shook hands. Aunt Kathy put her arm around Teresa and led her toward the house. Uncle Pat was evidently trying to make Tomasito laugh, but the boy did not understand what he said and was indeed confused by all the hubbub and excitement. Jack's nephew, a boy about nine, was evidently named Johnnie. When they reached the house he was introduced to two younger children, Sharon, a girl of five, and a little boy, Timmy, who was a two-year-old.

"Where are the llamas?" asked Johnnie suddenly.

"The llamas!" exclaimed Jack. "I almost forgot them. Tommy," he said in Spanish, "we must take the llamas to the barn."

The whole family filed out to the truck to see the strange creatures from South America.

"Let me help unload them!" cried Johnnie.

"No, Johnnie," Jack said. "Tommy is the only one who can handle the llamas." But the minute Jack let down the tailgate, Johnnie jumped in the truck and began to pull and tug on Allca's fur.

"*Cuidado!*" shouted Tomasito.

"Get down from there, Johnnie!" yelled Uncle Pat. But it was too late. The frightened llama turned his head and spat. Poor Johnnie fled to the house, followed by his mother.

Later, his sister told him that the Peruvian boy had made a small clicking sound and that the llamas had walked out of the truck and toward the barn as if they had always known the way. "Just like magic," she said.

After Tomasito had bedded down the llamas in their new home, he returned to Uncle Pat's house. It was full of bright lights and many voices seeming to talk at once. Tomasito and Teresa were relieved when Jack finally rose and said to them in Spanish, "Now we will go to *our* house. Pat has fixed up my father's old place for us."

Uncle Pat's family conducted them across the driveway to a modest, box-like house with an old-fashioned porch, its fresh paint gleaming under the new floodlight. The front door was narrow and on either side of it was a prim little window dressed in fresh white curtains. Uncle Pat unlocked the door. Just as they were about to step inside Jack stopped, looked fondly at Teresa, then picked her up in his arms.

"This is what we do in the United States when a bride enters her first home," he said. "This is our first home!" And he kissed her.

After all the good-nights had been said, Tomasito found himself in a bedroom of his own. Teresa helped him to unpack and arrange his clothes.

"See," she said. "Here is your desk, to use when you are a student."

Tomasito immediately placed on it the book and the precious llama Don Pedro had given him. Teresa smiled and hugged him. "Don Pedro will be proud of you," she murmured.

It was good to have Teresa with him, talking to him in

74

Quechua. But soon he must say good night to her. He felt lonely as he looked at the smooth, square bed.

"Would Señor Jack be offended if I slept with the llamas?" he asked. "It is a strange place for them."

Teresa looked at her young brother. Understanding and a little sadness were in her eyes. "I think if we tell him you want to calm them down he will understand. I'll ask him."

She came back a few minutes later with a flashlight and a sleeping bag. "Jack says to be sure that contrary Allca gets a good night's sleep," she laughed. "Good night to you, my brother."

Tomasito raced for the barn, never stopping to turn on the flashlight. Inside, he went straight to his friends. He patted and talked to each one, then lay down in the straw next to Allca.

"Allca, dear friend," he said, "you must be good now and do your work. I must work hard too. We must make Papá proud!"

Work

As TOMASITO awoke the next morning, for the first time in weeks he could hear only the sounds of nature—birds and the sighing of wind in the pine trees. He opened his eyes. Sunlight streamed through a small window above him and he could see a patch of vivid blue sky. Allca was lying on the straw beside him and Kuzni, Puca, and Quilla were quietly munching hay in their stalls nearby.

The barn looked almost as sturdy as the Inca house at home, but it was much more spacious. Jack had once told Tomasito that his father had owned a small dairy, and this barn, built of basalt blocks, had been the winter home of his herd. When Mr. and Mrs. McGerraghty moved to a warmer climate, neither of their sons had been interested in the dairy so the herd had been sold and the barn had lain unused. It was full of dust, cobwebs, and mouldy hay, but its walls were still strong and tight. Tomasito could visualize a veritable palace for his animals, once he had cleaned out all the dust and debris.

He was wide awake now and eager to explore the outdoors. He found that the barn, the old ranch house, and Uncle Pat's house stood on a sandy flat among widely spaced pines and other conifers. The corral outside the barn faced to the north and was built on a lush mountain meadow, a flat expanse of emerald grass which stretched for a mile or so westward from the road. In the distance Tomasito could see the great range of snow-capped mountains which, the day before, had so lifted his heart.

"Tomasito! Tomasito!"

He turned to greet Teresa, coming toward him from the barn.

"*Ay*, my sister, did you see the mountains?"

Teresa seemed to have taken on new life in the clear mountain air. "Come now for breakfast, my brother," she commanded. "I cooked it myself and Jack is hungry."

Jack was already seated at the breakfast table in the kitchen. Before him were platters of steaming food, both Peruvian and North American. He looked very proud and was already enthusiastically serving himself from the various dishes.

"Well, Tommy, how goes it? I hope the llamas were able to sleep in their new barn. How do you like my mountains?"

"*Magníficas*, Señor Jack!" exclaimed Tomasito.

"Today," Jack said, as soon as Tomasito had taken his place at the table, "I must go down with Uncle Pat to his office on the lake to discuss business. While I am there, I'll try to get wind of a rig for the llama rides. Maybe we could even use three other animals. How about adding Shetland ponies or burros?"

"Burros might be best, Señor Jack. The llamas are used to them."

"Very well, then," continued Jack. "While I'm gone, look around the place. See if the pasture fences are intact so that we can let the animals browse without a herder when you go to

77

school. Johnnie will show you how far our place extends. You'll have to show him how to make up to Allca, though. I think he learned his lesson about llamas!" He laughed as he rose from the table to give his wife a good-by kiss.

"Haven't had such a good breakfast in years!" he told her. "Kathy will be over shortly to show you around town—what there is of it. Pat and I may not be back till six or so."

For Tomasito the following days were filled with hard but happy work. Jack and Uncle Pat returned one day from Tahoe with a turnstile and three burros. The burros looked rather worn and flea-bitten, but after Tomasito had curried and petted them and let them feed for a few days in the lush meadow, they began to take on a more presentable appearance.

Tomasito had cleaned the barn until it shone. "How many families might be happy in such a warm, clean house!" Tomasito and Teresa thought sadly.

Tomasito found young Johnnie McGerraghty to be something of a problem. He had given the llamas a wide berth since the night of their arrival, but after awhile he began to demand that he be allowed to play with them. The boy from Peru did not know what to make of children who were so forward. Where he came from the younger children respected not only adults but their elder brothers and cousins as well. This brash youngster seemed to have no respect for anything.

Finally, however, Tomasito found something which a North American boy did seem to respect—skill. For some time Johnnie had been baffled by the magical manner in which Tomasito guided the llamas. One day the two boys set out to explore the upland portions of the McGerraghty ranch and Tomasito took his llamas along. As usual, they strode ahead of him calmly as he guided them with sounds that were barely perceptible to the human ear.

"Teach me how to herd them!" begged Johnnie.

"Very difficult to teach," objected Tomasito, who really hadn't any idea how one could. But Johnnie listened attentively and finally began to hear the signals more accurately. He began to try to imitate the clicks and whistles.

"No! Like this!" Tomasito repeated one of the sounds. Johnnie tried again, but Tomasito shook his head and the llamas paid no attention at all.

After that, whenever he found Tomasito with the llamas, Johnnie continued to practice. One day Tomasito said, "Good, Johnnie. That's better. You must be friends with the animals," he went on. "Must love them. Here, make friends with Kuzni. Love him, don't scare him." It was very hard to explain what he meant in English. Finally, he separated Kuzni from the others and let Johnnie pet him and play with him in the corral.

In time, Johnnie began to imitate the older boy in other ways and gradually grew more gentle in manner. Tomasito observed with pleasure that a friendly relationship was starting to grow up between the boy and Kuzni.

Johnnie was an enthusiastic guide. He hiked with Tomasito into Parson's Flat and presented him to Mr. Sorenson, the storekeeper, to Mr. Buffer, the manager of the Sierra Motel, and to Mr. Moss, the sheriff.

"But where is the teacher?" asked Tomasito, somewhat anxiously, after these introductions.

"Well," answered Johnnie, "the school is about a mile out of town. It's a unified school so there are five teachers. But we're having vacation now so the teachers are at home. We'll probably see them at the store sooner or later. Let's go down to the creek."

Johnnie led the way down a flowery bank to a noisy mountain stream. To Tomasito the sound of the rushing water seemed a

79

faint echo of the Urubamba and he stared happily at the silvery rapids, his mind filled with images of his ancient home.

Although Johnnie was a good guide, he showed no inclination toward other work. Often he disappeared with other boys his age into the mountains and canyons near the town, reappearing only now and then for meals. Tomasito would have expected a nine-year-old in Peru to help him set up the llama rides, but in a way he was glad that the impetuous boy was out of his way most of the time.

Jack and his brother Pat were gone all day long, so that, once basic decisions had been made as to just where the rides should be set up, Tomasito was left to get everything in order. They had found a lovely spot near the highway, beneath the pines, where the children could ride in the shade. Tomasito sanded and oiled the turnstile and painted its spokes with the gaily colored paints Teresa had helped him pick out at the store. Jack was very pleased.

"All we need now are some signs," he said to Tomasito. "I'll have them made in Bijou."

"Before we put them up I must train the animals, Señor Jack."

"Well, I guess that's right," agreed Jack. "We don't want that Allca playing any tricks on us."

So Tomasito set out to train the llamas. The burros were a help, as they were already used to the job. The three male llamas proved surprisingly cooperative. They had never been ridden before but they had carried bundles of fodder and provisions. They seemed only a little confused by the saddles, the turnstile, and by the squealing children. To their delight, Sharon and Timmy were given endless free rides as "trainers," and soon other children from the town came to lend their services. Tomasito had to appeal to Aunt Kathy to explain that no children over five were allowed to ride.

One afternoon Johnnie and another husky nine-year-old named Steve stopped by to see what was going on.

"Let's have a ride," suggested Johnnie, approaching Kuzni and Puca.

"No! No! Too big!" protested Tomasito. But before he was able to stop them, the two boys had swung into the saddles. They kicked the animals as they would have their ponies, and yelled at them to go. Kuzni was the first to respond. He moved ahead a few steps and then stopped. The heavy load and noisy thumping seemed to confuse him. Suddenly he folded his legs under him and sat down—the ancient llama protest against insufferable conditions. As Kuzni pulled down on an arm of the rig, the whole apparatus creaked and groaned, animals strained in their harnesses, straps became tangled and torn, burros brayed, and the boys yelled more loudly than ever.

It was some time before boys and animals were untangled. Johnnie and Steve did help straighten out the harnesses, keeping, as Tomasito observed, one eye on the house, then sheepishly mounted their bicycles and pedalled quickly out of sight.

Tomasito was left with two little girls who kept squealing and asking him questions while he surveyed the damage. It was very discouraging. None of the spokes of the rig had been broken but there would be harnesses to mend before they could open the rides to the public. Most important of all, how would Kuzni and Puca respond to the next riders? The little girls finally went away and Tomasito glumly unhitched the animals to take them to the corral.

He went into the barn and lay down in the hay in the loft. Inside his head his thoughts thrashed angrily about. He hated these North American brats, insolent and lazy! Why should he, almost a grown man, have to coddle giggling little girls? There wasn't even anybody to talk to. Of course he would not tattle to

81

Jack or Uncle Pat or run whimpering to his sister. He wished his brother Pablo were here—or that he had a friend of his own.

As Tomasito looked absently around the loft, his gaze was arrested by a curved object he had not noticed before and which he could now see dimly by the light shining through the haymow door. Could it be a sickle? It was! Now he could cut hay for the winter!

Tomasito had been worrying about winter feed for the llamas ever since his arrival. The McGerraghty ranch would produce a fine crop of wild hay later on and if he could manage to cut it before the winter rains and snow set in, Jack would not have to pay for fodder.

While cleaning the barn Tomasito had come across a scythe which he knew had once been used to cut hay. But it was now heavy with rust and when he tried swinging it he found that he could hardly lift it, much less control the long handle and heavy blade. In his country, where the fields were small and uneven, sickles were used to harvest grains. Now he had his sickle! He examined it carefully. It too was crusty with rust and dirt but perhaps Mr. Sorenson could clean and sharpen it for him.

In a few days the harnesses were repaired and the rig back in operation. The llamas and burros knew their jobs well enough by now so that Tomasito could announce to Jack, "I think we could open the rides, Señor Jack."

"Good," Jack answered. "Let's put up the signs tonight so that you can be ready for business tomorrow."

The two went to the barn for the signs which Jack had ordered. They put one on the western side of the highway to attract travelers from Lake Tahoe. "LLAMA and BURRO RIDES— 100 YARDS," it read. On the eastern side, facing motorists coming from Calaveras, they posted a similar sign, with an arrow pointing across the road. To a tree near the rides they fastened a board which announced:

LLAMA and BURRO RIDES

10 min.—25¢

NO children over 5 years of AGE

Jack gave Tomasito a change dispenser to wear on his belt. "Here is five dollars in change to start with," he said. "Perhaps you'd better practice with Teresa so you won't get mixed up tomorrow."

So Tomasito and Teresa rehearsed. Teresa gave her brother various denominations of money, one-dollar and five-dollar bills and various coins, and Tomasito made change. He had bought things at Mr. Sorenson's store and was familiar with American currency, but when he thought of making change for six different riders at once he grew nervous.

"Just take it easy," advised Jack. "Remember, children aren't in that much of a hurry. Just take your time and make sure you give the right change. Be sure everybody stays behind the rope while you put each child in the saddle. Then nobody will get hurt."

Tomasito didn't sleep much that night, thinking of all his responsibilities. But morning finally came and after breakfast the well-groomed little animals were hitched to the shiny turnstile, a llama alternating with a burro. There they stood, under the pine trees, waiting for riders.

Tomasito was tense as he looked up and down the highway. Johnnie and his friend Steve came by on their bikes on their way to town.

"Don't worry, Tommy," they reassured him, seeing his anxious face. "It's only eight-thirty. Tourists don't generally get going this early. We'll tell Mr. Sorenson and the Buffers that you're open." And they set off.

Tomasito grew tired of standing, straining first in one direction, then the other, as he heard approaching cars. Sometimes the cars or trucks contained people he knew—Mr. Sorenson's son bringing supplies from Lake Tahoe, Mr. Buffer going to pick up a parcel at the airport. The drivers waved at him and called, "Good luck, Tommy!" But nobody stopped. Not all morning.

Teresa came at noon and Tomasito told her the sad news. "Nobody has stopped. Not a single car. Perhaps nobody will ever stop and Jack will sell the llamas!"

"But no, my brother," she protested, speaking comfortingly to him in Quechua. "You know from the ruins that tourists are very lazy. They like to sleep late. Maybe they just don't get this far till afternoon. Come, have some lunch."

"I can't leave the animals. Somebody might come while I'm gone."

"But you have to eat, Tomasito. I'll send Sharon down to watch while you have lunch."

Tomasito finally consented. Sharon came and sat under the tree. "*Hijita*," Tomasito admonished her as he left, "tell people you call me."

He gulped down the soup Teresa had prepared and listened for the sound of motors. Finally a car stopped. Its door slammed and Tomasito dashed out the kitchen door and around the house. But before he could reach the front porch he heard the car drive away.

Sharon was running toward the house, crying, "I said, 'Please wait,' but they left anyway."

Tomasito leaned against the trunk of the pine tree and stared into the sky. After awhile he unhitched the animals and led them to drink from the brook. Sharon silently helped, managing to unfasten one of the burros by herself. After all the animals

84

had been watered, she said, "Let me ride, Tommy. Then the animals won't forget how."

Tomasito smiled bitterly. "Okay," he said, lifting her onto Puca. He started the circle going, walking listlessly beside the llamas.

"Somebody's stopped!" whispered Sharon excitedly. "Look!" It was true. A station wagon had left the road and pulled up near them. Three young children climbed over the tailgate. "See, Daddy! The man in the gas station was right. They *are* llamas!" happily observed one of the little boys.

"So they are," agreed his father. "Now which animal do you want to ride, Rich?"

"A llama!"

"And Stan? And Suzy?"

"Llamas!" they both yelled.

"But one of the llamas is taken."

Tomasito finally resolved the dilemma by helping Sharon to dismount. "Her ride all gone," he explained.

Somehow Tomasito managed to make change, put the children on the animals, start the rides, and stop them at the proper time. What triumph he felt when, at the end of the first ten minutes, the children persuaded their parents to let them have another ride and more silver coins fell into the change dispenser. When the car left at last, Sharon jumped up and down and hugged Tomasito.

But no more customers came that day.

When Jack and Pat came home that night, Tomasito recounted with some embarrassment the one event of the day and gave Jack the small handful of coins. Jack patted him on the shoulder. "Good boy! We're in business!"

Tomasito was shocked. "But only one car came, Señor Jack!"

"Word has to get around, Tommy," Uncle Pat said encourag-

85

ingly. "Your first customers are probably talking about the llamas right now. The news has to spread. You'll see—pretty soon people will even be coming up from Lake Tahoe just to show the kids the llamas."

"The season hasn't really started yet, either," added Jack. "Next week should be livelier. The Fourth of July falls on the following Monday so people will be coming for the long week-end."

"Fourth of July?" inquired Tomasito.

"Independence Day, our big national holiday, Tommy," Jack explained. "People like to start their vacations that week, especially when the holiday adds to the weekend."

Jack was right. Only a few cars stopped each day that first week. But Tomasito knew that word of the llamas was spreading; parents were bringing their children to Parson's Flat from as far away as Bijou and Stateline.

The week of July Fourth brought a stream of tourists—occupants of the cabins along the river, visitors to the new state park, sightseers who had driven the scenic route of the Big Trees and high passes on their way to Lake Tahoe. Tomasito was busy indeed. Sometimes children had to wait for rides. Fortunately, Sharon rose to the occasion and helped line them up, keeping track of whose turn was next. On one or two days they had to close down the rides for half an hour in the middle of the day to give the animals a rest.

As the weeks of summer went by, business continued to be good. Jack was pleased with Tomasito's hard work and also with the amount of money he was earning. In the evenings the men would discuss with Tomasito the events of the day and help him work out business problems. Tomasito was proud to have a business of his own. He felt very adult.

The fame of the llamas spread, not only among the tourists,

86

but among the people of the countryside. Ranchers, highway workers, rangers, and guides, coming into Parson's Flat for supplies, would bring their children for a ride or a look at the strange animals. Children old enough to come on their own were regular spectators. Most of them watched respectfully from a distance. Once, when a bigger boy threatened to push his way in, Sharon told him, "You'd better not do that. Those llamas get mean when you're rough with them. Once Allca there spit right into a boy's face!"

One day a whole procession of cars stopped, one after the other. Children were lined up waiting their turn and Tomasito had to work as fast as he could to get the children in and out of the saddles. His back was tired from lifting them and his feet ached from walking in a circle. In the background were the usual local boys and girls who merely came to look. Tomasito had no time even to nod to those he knew. Presently he saw a boy of his own age leaning against a pine tree, watching quietly. Tomasito was startled. The boy's face could have been that of his cousin in Pisac. A Peruvian face?

Tomasito had no time for further reflection. More and more children pressed against the rope. Suddenly he was aware that someone was lifting a child down from one of the burros. It was the boy from the pine tree.

Throughout the rest of the afternoon the strange boy with the dark oval face and jet-black eyes worked beside Tomasito, lifting children down, lifting others up, watching silently as Tomasito marched patiently around and around to keep the animals moving.

Five o'clock came at last, the hour which Jack had agreed should be the end of the working day. The "Closed" sign had discouraged a few late-comers and the last customers finally climbed into their cars and drove away. Sharon immediately headed for home. Tomasito, so tired he could scarcely see, was surprised to find that the boy with the Peruvian face was still there. He was unsaddling one of the burros.

"Thanks," Tomasito said in Quechua. "Who are you?" The boy obviously did not understand, but he smiled.

"Thank you. Who are you?" repeated Tomasito in English.

"Joe," replied the boy. "Joe Henry."

Joe went on unhitching the animals. The two boys grinned shyly at each other as they worked. Joe led the burros back to the corral while Tomasito herded the llamas.

"Thanks, much thanks!" offered Tomasito as Joe was about to leave.

"I had fun," replied Joe. "I'll come back tomorrow." Then he walked off toward the road.

Tomasito watched him until he was out of sight. Who was Joe? He was not a Peruvian. But why did he look so familiar? And why had he helped? Tomasito began to think of the spirit stories of Tío Dominguez but then contented himself with the thought, "I wished for work and I wished for a friend. The children have come to ride the llamas and now Joe has come, too. Perhaps to be a friend."

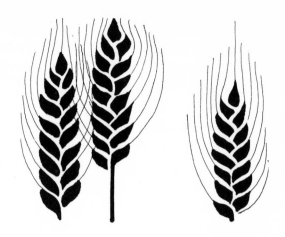

Joe

THE next day, as Tomasito drove the animals toward the turnstile, he looked eagerly ahead to see if Joe had come as promised. But he was not there.

"I wish Joe would come back," sighed Sharon. "When he helped load, the children didn't get so fidgety."

It was a busy day. The tourists began stopping early. By ten o'clock Tomasito and Sharon were working as fast as they could. Suddenly Sharon called, "Hi, Joe! Are we glad to see you!"

Tomasito looked up to see Joe, busy with the animal on the far side of the rig. The two boys nodded and smiled at each other, but there was no time for talk. Joe worked beside him steadily. Tomasito was less tired now that Joe was helping and the rides went more smoothly because it took so much less time to change riders.

At noon they closed the turnstile to rest and water the animals and to eat lunch.

"Come eat with me," invited Tomasito.

"No, I'd better go home," Joe protested.

"Please!" urged Tomasito. "We can talk." Finally Joe followed Tomasito to the house. "My friend Joe," Tomasito said proudly, presenting him to Teresa.

Teresa was delighted to have another hungry boy to feed and Joe proved to be the most appreciative boarder she had had. He was persuaded to eat plate after plate of Peruvian stew.

The proposed talk seemed destined for postponement, however. Joe's quiet manner, Tomasito's and Teresa's meagre English, and the enthusiasm of all for the stew, prevented any real conversation. Finally Joe volunteered that he lived down by the river, had heard of the animals, and had come to take a look at them. "I like the llamas," he said. "The burros too. It's fun helping. I'll come each day if you want me." Tomasito learned that Joe was his same age and went to the unified school. This was a start toward friendship.

Tomasito still longed for a chance to really talk to Joe, but July was the height of the tourist season and they were busy all day long. Teresa insisted that Joe come for lunch regularly and each day he and Tomasito added a few bits to the knowledge they had of each other. One day, when the boys came back from lunch, they found a chill wind whipping the pine branches and rolling great dark clouds overhead.

"Guess we're in for a storm," observed Joe. Even as he said this, plump drops began to make craters in the sandy soil. "There won't be any children coming to ride the llamas for an hour or so at least. Should we take the animals to the barn?"

"Okay," replied Tomasito.

Inside the barn the boys leaned comfortably against a bale of hay and listened to the roar of the thunder and the gusts of rain against the window. It didn't seem so hard to talk here, and

90

they began to tell each other some of the important things in their lives—about their families, their interests, their ambitions. Tomasito delighted in talking about his father and Pablo and Jacinto and the girls, and even about Tío Dominguez. Joe told about his ancient grandmother who talked to him about the spirits and about Uncle Joe who had gone away to the university.

Joe listened intently to Tomasito's description of Don Pedro and of their work among the ruins. But when Tomasito spoke enthusiastically of beginning school in the fall and of learning history and mathematics and science, Joe obviously lost interest.

"Don't you like school, Joe?" inquired Tomasito.

"School's all right. The new school's got a real good baseball diamond. Maybe we could walk up there sometime and I'll show you. Can you play baseball?"

"No," answered Tomasito. "Jack lets me watch with him on TV, but I never played."

"That's okay. We don't play baseball till spring. Maybe I can teach you by then. In the fall we play football. Can you play that?"

"I play *futból*, but Jack says it's not the same game. Do all the boys play here?"

"Oh, we practice," replied Joe. "But only the high school has a team. Same with basketball. We don't have a gym at school, but we practice when there's not too much snow on the playground."

"We love basketball in Peru. Many good teams."

When they had exhausted the topic of sports, Tomasito began to tell Joe about the llama rides. "They must pay for my food and clothes. Now we take in lots of money and Jack is pleased. But soon winter comes. The tourists go home. I go to school. No money. Besides, when snow comes, Jack must buy fodder."

He then showed Joe the sickle and the scythe. "If I could

91

sharpen the little one, I could cut hay for winter. Big one better, but too big for me."

"I think my father could sharpen them for you," offered Joe. "He might be able to show you how to use the scythe. He cuts weeds sometimes for the Highway Department. The hay will soon be ready to cut. Ask Mr. McGerraghty if you can come down to my house after dinner tomorrow night. I'll come get you."

How much easier everything was when you had a friend! Tomasito was filled with warmth and hope as he ate supper that night. He could hardly wait for the meal to be finished and for the time to come when he, Jack, Pat, and Johnnie would sit together and discuss the day's business.

At last, after they were seated in the kitchen and had talked of the weather and the various ways the storm had interfered with their affairs, Tomasito related his experience. "My friend Joe and I talk long time in barn. Joe says his papa will sharpen my sickle so I can cut hay for winter. May I go to Joe's house tomorrow night, Señor Jack?"

"Who's Joe?" asked Jack, curious to know how Tomasito, working so continuously, had managed to make a friend.

"Joe help me with llama rides. We talk a little at lunch. He help a lot so children no have to wait."

"You mean he helps you every day and Teresa feeds him?"

"Oh, yes! Joe very hungry," agreed Teresa warmly.

"Well, who is this operator? Do you know him, Pat?"

"It's Joe Henry," volunteered Johnnie.

"He's an Indian kid from down by the river," added Pat. "Maybe you remember his father, Sam Henry. Or old Granny Henry we kids used to think was a witch?"

"Sure, I remember them. Sam was a real tough guy, for an Indian. But you couldn't trust any of 'em—steal the shirt off your

92

back. Tommy, I don't want any of those Indians hanging around the place! Do you understand? Especially with Pat and me gone all day."

There was a stunned silence.

"We are Indians too, my husband," said a cold, hard voice at last. Jack saw before him, not the warm, gentle faces of his wife and her brother, but two masks, hard and cold as obsidian. The image of a Peruvian village he had once visited flashed through his mind. He recalled its street lined with these bitter faces, the walls inscribed with legends of hatred and despair: "Down with the Government! Out with the Yankees!"

Finally Jack rose and went into the living room. He turned the knob of the television set, sat down, and gazed unhappily at the screen. Pat sat down near him.

"Things are changing, Jack. The Indian kids are going through school and getting jobs just like anybody else now. Of course a lot of them are poor. But I don't think they steal."

"Joe Henry's a real good guy," added Johnnie, who had joined them. "He gets bad grades in school but, boy, can he ever play baseball!"

Jack said nothing in reply. All three stared at the television screen in order to avoid looking at each other.

No sound came from the kitchen. Tomasito stayed with his sister until she had finished doing the dishes. Then he opened the back door and they stepped outside.

"We will not send Joe away!" Teresa said in Quechua. "He is our friend!"

"But Jack is your husband," Tomasito replied bitterly.

"My husband will not offend an Indian!" insisted Teresa with a conviction which astonished her brother. "So don't send Joe away tomorrow. See that he comes here to lunch. And tell him we'll bring that sickle to his father, even if we can't bring it

93

tomorrow evening." Her black eyes were fierce. "Good night, my brother. Don't forget."

Tomasito, who had continued to sleep with the llamas in the stone barn where he felt more at home, waited until Jack had gone the next morning before he entered the house. He looked anxiously at Teresa. Her face was sober but proud. She had prepared an especially good breakfast for him and waited on him as though he were the man of the house. Before Tomasito left for work, she reminded him, "Remember, my brother, greet your friend Joe as always and be sure to invite him to lunch."

Tomasito looked dubious as he went out to hitch up the animals. Soon Sharon appeared, then Joe. It was a busy morning and Tomasito had little time to think of the lunch hour. It came all too soon, however, and they were a little late in unharnessing the animals. When they had finished they saw Teresa coming toward them from the house. "You are late," she said cheerfully. "I have real good stew today." And she gave them a warm and welcoming smile.

Teresa, who usually spoke little at lunch time, now took over the conversation. She asked the boys about the various animals and told them she had been out to the corral to visit Quilla. Then she asked Tomasito about his plans for harvesting the hay. "I can use a sickle, so I could harvest too," she said.

"Maybe I could find somebody who would loan one. But most of the harvesting is done here by machine now," Joe answered.

And so the lunch hour passed without awkwardness.

The afternoon was as busy as the morning. Tomasito, Joe, and Sharon worked hard. Suddenly, about four o'clock, Sharon said, "Why, there's Daddy and Uncle Jack!" Tomasito froze.

Jack and Pat had pulled in along side of the customers' cars and were watching the operation of the rides. Tomasito felt cold and shaky inside, but he kept working as usual. So did Joe.

After what seemed like a very long time, the two men got out of the car and started over toward the children. Pat introduced Joe. "This is Joe Henry, Tommy's friend."

"Hi!" Jack replied briefly. Then he waited for Tomasito, making the circle with Allca, to pass him. "If you kids are going to take those tools down to Joe's tonight, you'd better knock off in a few minutes." With that, he put up the "Closed" sign on the tree. "Next ride's the last one," he announced to the people waiting.

"You're doing fine, Sharon," praised her father. The two men got back into their car and drove toward the house.

While he was washing up for dinner Tomasito was able to exchange a few private words with Teresa.

"Jack said I could take the tools to Joe's. I wonder what made him change?"

"Jack spoke without knowing," replied Teresa, a faint smile on her lips. "He didn't really know the Indians when he was a boy. And he forgot how much has happened since then." Tomasito wasn't sure exactly what she meant but he gathered that his friendship with Joe was safe. However, his anger at Jack was still strong.

Tomasito was silent during the meal. Jack did not address him, but instead related to Teresa the trouble he and Pat had had with the wiring of a new winter resort being built near the new state park. Tomasito excused himself before dessert and went out to the pasture to check the llamas.

When he returned, Joe was waiting for him at the barn. "It's okay," announced Joe. "My father says he will sharpen the tools for you. Here, I'll carry the scythe for awhile and then we'll trade."

95

Tomasito followed across the pasture to the river, along the river for a distance, and under the highway bridge to the east of the town. Tomasito noticed a number of dwellings in the river valley, a few built on ledges in the valley wall, and one or two more in the pine woods on top of the bluff. Joe took a path leading to the high ground.

Tomasito looked in dismay at the homes of the Indians. It was not that they were much different from Indian homes along the Urubamba—small, simple constructions of wood and pieces of old metal instead of mud, stone, and thatch. But there were lights in the windows and television aerials on every roof. It was just that these houses, small, unpainted, and fragile-looking, contrasted so sharply with the neat, solid, cheerfully painted homes in the rest of Parson's Flat. They somehow reminded him of Jack's words the night before. Tomasito felt confused and uncomfortable.

As they reached the top of the bluff, Tomasito saw a clearing in the forest. To one side of it, near the bluff, were two small houses like those in the river bottom. The clearing itself was filled with old battered automobiles, most without wheels, some without doors, hoods, or fenders. In one corner of the clearing was a pile of metal from the car bodies, flattened and bent to a common size.

The house which they were approaching was encased in the same scrap metal and had a steep scrap-metal roof from which a TV antenna extended. The variegated colors of the metal, taken from different car bodies, acted as a camouflage, so that the house almost disappeared in the moving shadows of the pines.

The boys leaned the tools against the house and entered the living room, remarkably tidy but lined with gear—snowshoes, fishing rods, tools of various kinds—and dominated by

96

a television set which occupied most of one wall. Opposite the TV, in an old armchair, sat Joe's father, staring into the set. Mrs. Henry, seated on a metal cot, was diligently sewing. As the boys entered, Mr. Henry passed his hand across his face as if to brush away lines of fatigue. He smiled as Joe said, "Here's Tommy, Dad. And this is my mother."

"We're glad to see you, Tommy." Joe's mother smiled too. Her voice was quiet and gentle. Both Joe's parents had the dark, oval faces, wide at the cheek-bones, and the black eyes which made Tomasito feel as if he had seen them before.

"Come outside, boys," said Mr. Henry, "and let's see if we can fix up those tools. They really need it, don't they!" he exclaimed. "Mr. McGerraghty senior moved away quite a few years ago and I guess he hadn't used them for a long time before that. But I think we can grind off that rust."

He led the boys to the rear of the house where a grindstone stood on the back porch. After they had brought it out into an open space, Mr. Henry said, "Let's try the sickle first. Joe, you turn the handle. Tommy, here's a can of water. When I tell you, pour some on the stone. I'll hold the sickle."

They started to work and little by little the rusty blade was burnished and honed until it was a circle of bright steel. Tomasito could feel its sharpness as he pressed his thumb against the blade, and he laughed to see the head of a weed separate from the stem when the edge of the blade touched it.

"Now for the scythe." This was harder work and Tomasito could see the lines of fatigue growing deeper around Mr. Henry's eyes. But finally the task was done.

"When are you going to cut the hay, Tommy?" asked Mr. Henry. "It's getting pretty ripe now."

"Weekend no good," replied Tomasito. "Too many tourists.

Not so many on Mondays. I get up early, real early. Perhaps I can cut much before breakfast."

"Fine, Tommy. I'll come over Monday morning and show you how to use the scythe. It's too late tonight. Come now, I'll take you home." Mr. Henry led the way to an old pickup truck and placed the tools in the back.

That night Tomasito moved his sleeping bag so that he could see his tools with their shining blades reflected on the barn wall. He would show Jack that he could take care of his llamas even in the winter!

Sunday night Tomasito hardly slept at all. He kept planning and replanning his attack on the meadow. The grass, so lush and green in June, had turned to golden fur. There was a beautiful crop of hay in the vast meadow. How many days would it take him to cut it? Could he bring the hay in by himself before another storm came along? But he could face these difficulties as he imagined the loft piled with the sweet-smelling fodder.

At last the dawn came. Tomasito led the llamas into the pasture for their breakfast. He returned to the barn and, almost trembling with excitement, lifted down the great scythe. He just had to try it, even though Mr. Henry was not there to show him how to use it. Very carefully, to avoid stumbling in the dim light, he picked his way through the corral, across the pasture where the llamas were munching their morning meal, and into the furry expanse of the great meadow. The hay, still wet on top from the dew, was up to his knees. "I'll start right here," he thought, "Then I can see Mr. Henry when he comes."

Just then, the burning rim of the sun moved up over the crest of the mountains, their ridges purple against a green-gold sky. The boy stood still, for a moment sensing the reverence his ancestors must have felt for the Sun God, giver of warmth and life. Then he placed the great curved blade among the stalks of hay and began to swing. The first stroke was clumsy. The blade got caught in some stems and slid over others, leaving a ragged stubble. He brought the heavy scythe back to the right and swung again. This time he nearly lurched forward onto the tool; the point had caught on the fence post. But he backed up and swung once more.

"Not bad at all, Tommy," said a voice. "Maybe you don't need us." Mr. Henry and Joe were smiling at him over the fence. Each had a scythe over his shoulder.

"We borrowed these from the Highway Department," explained Mr. Henry. "Now I can teach you and Joe at the same time. I'll work in front and each of you work a row behind. Be sure you are staggered so nobody will lose a leg."

"Before you start, *señores*, here is chocolate." It was Teresa, carrying a sickle and a covered basket. She brought out a thermos jug and quickly poured a steaming cup of chocolate for each of them.

"My sister, Señora McGerraghty," Tomasito announced, introducing Teresa to Mr. Henry. "I told her, Señor Henry, that you would come to show me how to use the big scythe. How did you know, Teresa, that Joe would come?"

"I watch," laughed Teresa.

Tomasito noticed then that Teresa was wearing her Quechuan dress and shawl and was barefoot. She saw Tomasito looking at her feet.

"Feel so good!" she exclaimed, squeezing the grass stems with her toes. She put away the cups and thermos and took up the sickle.

"You use scythes but I can use this," she said cheerfully.

99

She began to mow the hay to the right of the gate, drawing the sickle skillfully in smooth, even curves. Mr. Henry smiled.

"Let's get to work, boys, or Mrs. McGerraghty will have the field all mowed!" He set out eastward across the meadow, his scythe moving in slow, stately measures. The two boys followed behind him, first Tomasito and then Joe, and soon they too were caught up in the rhythm, almost carried along by the swoop of the blade. Back and forth, back and forth, they swung. Tomasito was so fascinated that he lost all track of time. Suddenly, as he approached the east fence, he noticed two men coming toward them. They were Jack and Pat. The sun was already quite high above the horizon. Teresa had disappeared.

"*Díos mío!*" exclaimed Jack. "Look what they've done!"

"Why, they've got a crew!" added Pat. "Hi, Sam! Do you remember my brother Jack? Jack, this is Joe's father. You knew him when we were kids."

"Hope you don't mind our mowing your hay. I promised to show Tommy how to use a scythe," explained Mr. Henry.

Jack didn't quite know what to say.

"Heck, no," he exclaimed at last. "Tommy is dead set on getting in this hay for the winter. I didn't really know what he was up to. Thanks for the help. My wife says it's breakfast time. You guys must be ready to quit by now."

Tomasito looked around. "When did Teresa go in? I no see her. Look how much!" He pointed at the wide stretch of meadow she had mowed.

"You mean my wife has been out here mowing too? Just wait till I see her!"

They all trooped into the kitchen where Teresa was dishing up sausages, fried potatoes, and a platter of eggs.

100

When breakfast was over, Jack turned to Teresa. "What do you mean, sneaking out to mow?" he demanded.

"Indian women can do that." Teresa smiled at him. "Work no hurt Indian women."

"None of that now!" scolded Jack. "Too much work is just as hard on Indian women as on any others, especially when they're pregnant. I want my wife and child to live a long time. Tommy, Teresa is going to have a baby in February and don't you dare plan any more outside jobs for her. In California we try to take special care of women expecting babies. No more haying, eh?"

Presently Pat, who had gone back to his own house for breakfast, came by to pick up Jack. Johnnie was with him, very much impressed with the mowing.

"Pat," inquired Jack, "couldn't we get Phil Daniels to bring his machine and mow the rest of the meadow and bale that hay? I can see Tommy's determined to get it into the barn. This way he's going to kill himself with work."

"The trouble is, everybody's mowing this week. I know Phil's all booked up till the end of the week."

"Do you think you and I could get off a little early tonight to help Tommy finish?" asked Jack.

"We can try. How had you planned to get the hay in, Tommy?"

"With the llamas," Tomasito answered. "Can carry big loads. Will work till dark."

"I know," spoke up Johnnie. "I can help. Because now I can drive Kuzni. I could load him and take him to the barn all by myself, couldn't I, Tommy?"

"Perhaps yes," agreed Tomasito. "Maybe we use the burros too."

Jack burst out laughing.

"Well, it sounds like a circus parade. But it just might work

101

—anything to get that hay off Tommy's mind and into the barn! Sam, could you work for us tonight, say from five on? Maybe you and Pat and I could mow enough to satisfy Tommy and the boys could stack it. Tommy, you boys could pile it up near the barn and Pat and I will see about getting it into the loft later on. We'd better get to work now, Pat. See you all tonight. Thanks a lot, Sam."

It was quite a scene that evening. Jack, Pat, and Mr. Henry mowed row after row of shining hay. After them moved an odd procession of boys and beasts. Johnnie, who had insisted that Tomasito teach him how to load Kuzni, proudly tied the bundles of hay on "his" llama and followed behind as the patient beast adroitly moved through gates and across fields in response to his commands. Johnnie was delighted to exhibit himself before an audience which had gathered along the fence.

Tomasito loaded and guided Allca and Puca. Joe followed with two burros. They worked until dark. It would take another night to finish the mowing, but there was already a good-sized haymow in the barnyard. Tomasito looked at it with pride.

"Satisfied, Tommy?" asked Jack presently, coming up behind him. "No danger now of losing the llamas during the winter!"

"No, *señor!*"

Tomasito beamed.

"But I must say," Jack continued, "you sure are a slave driver! Haven't worked so hard in years. I'll feel every muscle tomorrow—and I bet you'll be limber as a monkey!" He turned to Joe's father who had joined them. "It was good to work with you. Thanks for helping us out. Now, how much do we owe you?"

"Oh, nothing. Nothing at all, Jack. This was a little present to our friend, Tommy. You know, my brother says we Indians ought to work together more. Besides, I think Mrs. McGerraghty must have added a couple of inches to my boy with those lunches of hers. Hasn't she, Joe?"

The next Saturday night, after they had counted the week's receipts from the rides, Jack took Tomasito aside. "Tommy, you have been working very hard and you have earned a lot this summer. Right now you don't need much spending money, but in the fall there will be things you will want to buy. So maybe you had better save a little now. Every week I will give you ten dollars from the ride money."

Tomasito stared in amazement. "Ten dollars, for me?"

"Well, ten dollars may seem like a lot. Perhaps you don't need quite that much. But your helpers, Sharon and Joe, work hard too. Maybe you'd like to pay them. Sharon is so young she should only have a few dimes for her piggy bank. But Joe will be going to school in the fall and could use a few dollars. You could share whatever you want with him."

Later, Tomasito proudly paid Sharon a dollar in dimes. She jumped with delight, spilling the coins among the pine needles where the boys had to hunt for them. Joe didn't want to take the four dollars and fifty cents Tomasito handed him.

"I get a kick out of the animals," he said gruffly. "Besides, my Uncle Joe says we Indians need to learn to help each other out. Thanks anyway."

"But Jack said this is *my* money," Tomasito insisted. "I can share it if I want. Don Pedro told me Quechua Indians used to share everything. You share work, I share pay. Two ways for Indians to help. Okay?"

"Okay. Thanks, Indian." Joe took the money. The boys grinned at each other.

103

School

Not since the morning he had left home in Peru had Tomasito awakened in such a state of excitement. School! Today he would begin the studies which would enable him to work with Don Pedro. He had gone to school before, but this school would prepare him for high school and high school would prepare him for the University in Peru.

But what would school in California be like? Would the teacher be strict? How were you supposed to address him? Suppose the work was too hard? Thinking of these things, Tomasito stared out the window, forgetful of the clean clothes Teresa had laid out for him.

"Tomasito! Hurry! The bus will soon come!" Teresa's voice brought him back to the present moment.

Johnnie came by for him on the way to the bus stop. The two boys, carrying lunch boxes, went to stand by the mailboxes near the highway. "The bus driver's name is Myrtle and she talks cross," Johnnie offered. "My father calls her a battle-

axe. But she never does anything mean. Once when Rich
Masters' puppy got run over and Rich wouldn't get on the
bus till his mom could bandage the leg, Myrtle made a special
trip back for him. But she shouts at us if we even move in our
seats. Here she comes now!"

The big yellow bus rumbled across the cattle guard by the
bridge and swerved into the parking space that had been
used for the llama rides. Tomasito was glad he had been
warned about Myrtle. "Come on, Johnnie, don't dawdle now
or everybody'll be late! This your cousin? What's his name?
Tommy? Come on in, Tommy. Sit down there behind me
with Johnnie. And no changing seats, no standing up, no
fighting! Don't forget, now!" Tomasito was horrified.

Myrtle was a large, raw-boned woman with short gray hair.
Her glasses had enormous brown rims and were tinted yellow. Tomasito thought she looked very much like a huge owl.
Her large brown hands grasped the steering wheel firmly.
She would take no nonsense from the bus, either! Tomasito
suddenly felt amused. Without realizing it, he had begun to
smile. To his surprise, the owl's face, reflected in the rear-
view mirror, was smiling too.

Tomasito had been so anxious to obey Myrtle that he had
slid into his place without looking at the other children. So he
hadn't seen whether or not Joe was there. Now he didn't dare
turn around. He looked out the window on his side. It was a
beautiful fall day, every color and contour clean and bright as
though the landscape had prepared itself for this first day of
school. There had been a little frost over the weekend and the
aspen and willow trees along the river had begun to stand out
in gold against the evergreens.

The bus now turned eastward toward the river. The road

105

led through the familiar pine flats. Tomasito whispered to Johnnie, "Joe's house!"

"This is where most of the Indian kids get on," explained Johnnie.

The road made a loop near Joe's house. As they followed it, Tomasito caught sight of a double line of dark-skinned children of various ages, standing near a shelter made of old sheet metal. The children were lined up according to size, the young ones in front. It did not take Tomasito long to find Joe among the older children at the rear of the line. He wanted to call a greeting to him as he entered the bus but was afraid of Myrtle. Joe was looking for him, too, and they grinned at each other as Joe made his way to a rear seat.

It took Myrtle another half hour to pick up the town children. Whenever a new child got on, she asked his name and then warned him, as she had Tomasito, about what *not* to do on a school bus. Not many children looked scared, though.

"Next stop is the school," whispered Johnnie.

The bus crossed the river and climbed to a flat stretch of higher ground to the south of the town. It turned east again until it came to a broad, level stretch entirely cleared of trees. The school was new, a long gray-green box of a building. The United States flag, and below it the California Bear Flag, were flying from a tall flag pole in front. To the right was a large baseball field.

Myrtle drove the bus around to the rear of the building to unload. Here was an enormous clearing, laid bare by forest fires, part of which served as a playground. An evergreen forest surrounded three sides, but to the east, as far as the eye could see, were great stretches of misty meadows, the gray-blue mountains towering above them in the distance.

Tomasito thought, "I wish I didn't have to go into the

106

school. I wish I could just walk and walk with Allca and Quilla and Kuzni and Puca and look at the world."

But he had little time to wish. He suddenly found himself surrounded by children. Most of them had come to see the llamas at one time or another. Tomasito recognized some of them. He felt very shy at first, never having been the center of so much attention. But as the children asked him questions about the animals, he forgot his bashfulness and poor English and found himself talking quite freely.

An electric buzzer suddenly sounded and the children lined up before various entrances into the schoolhouse.

"I'm in the fifth grade this year, now that I'm almost ten," Johnnie told Tomasito. "But you'll be in the seventh. Uncle Jack said he talked to Mr. Thomas, the principal, so Mrs. Hohman, the seventh-grade teacher, knows you're coming. I'll introduce you to her."

Johnnie stood beside Tomasito and Joe in the seventh-grade line. Mrs. Hohman stood at the door and greeted each child as he entered. She was a grandmotherly looking woman with sad, empty eyes. She welcomed the children pleasantly, but Tomasito wondered if she really saw them. "It is almost as if she is a spirit already," he thought.

When Tomasito's turn came, Mrs. Hohman turned to Johnnie. "Oh, yes, the boy your Uncle Jack brought from Peru. Hello, Tomasito, I hope you'll get along all right." Then she added absently, "Strange to have Jack McGerraghty back. We thought we'd never see him again. He couldn't wait to get away. Maybe he thought we needed some foreign blood. You'd better sit in the front row. Over there on the right will be a good place. Just sit down. Thank you, Johnnie. You may go to your room now."

Tomasito watched Mrs. Hohman greet Joe. He hoped Joe

107

would sit near him but instead he quickly went to the back of the room. When all fifteen of the children had entered, Mrs. Hohman said in her pleasant but lifeless voice, "You are now in the seventh grade, boys and girls. I hope you will study hard so that next year you can graduate. First, let us pledge allegiance to the flag."

Tomasito did not know what "pledge allegiance" meant. He could neither understand the words nor why the children put their hands on their chests. But he stood up, put his hand on his chest too, and mumbled so that no one would notice him.

After the pledge of allegiance, Mrs. Hohman put some names on the blackboard. At the top of the list she wrote the word "Monitors." Two monitors were instructed to pass out the textbooks. Soon five thick books were piled on Tomasito's desk. He lifted their covers and glanced inside. He was filled with both delight and dismay. What beautiful pictures. What terrifying pages, full of unknown words. Why, he didn't know *any* of them!

Mrs. Hohman was pointing to a timetable on the blackboard. Tomasito listened to what she was saying and finally understood that the table showed what time the class would study various subjects during the day. Mathematics and Science and English he could understand, and Music and Art. The words were almost the same in Spanish. But what were Social Studies and Recess? Nevertheless, he was grateful for the time schedule and copied it carefully on one of the sheets of paper he had been given.

English was the first subject on the list. The children opened their books to a page which had lines like little street maps. On the lines were words. "This year," said Mrs. Hohman, "we are going to learn how to make pictures of sentences."

Tomasito could grasp some of the sentences: "The cat is black. The cat eats mice." But by the time he had figured out what the sentence meant, the class seemed to be talking about something else. When it came to the written exercises, he was hardly able to make a beginning before the period was over.

"Tomorrow we will have reading," announced Mrs. Hohman, holding up a book entitled *The Red Pony*. "Read pages one through ten before tomorrow."

Tomasito thought, "*The Red Pony*. I will like that."

Then came spelling. It was hard enough to learn what English words meant and how to say what you wanted to—but to *write* English! There were ten new words to learn. Tomorrow everybody must be able to write them correctly. Tomasito didn't understand any of the words—none of them were written the way they sounded.

And so it went throughout the day. Recess was a pleasant surprise and the lunch hour was fun. In the mathematics period in the afternoon Tomasito found that he could do some of the problems, but science and social studies contained for him only a miserable jumble of sounds and letters.

He was glad when a buzzer rang and Mrs. Hohman said, "Class dismissed." The children went to the cloakroom for their lunch boxes, then lined up by the bus.

"Sit by me this time," invited Joe as they entered the bus. Tomasito was pleased to be sitting in the back of the bus with the other big boys. He waved to Johnnie, who was also with a friend.

"How did you like our school, Tommy?" asked one of the boys from town.

109

"Okay. I like the boys and girls. But the lessons—very difficult. Too difficult for me!" Tomasito shook his head sadly.

"You'll get used to it," consoled the boy. "Mrs. Hohman's pretty easy. They say she doesn't pay much attention to you if you don't raise your hand or make a noise."

"What are you going to do when you get home, Tommy?" asked Joe.

"Take the llamas to the mountain. They need walk. Need hard grass so teeth not grow too long. Come with me," he added.

"I have to help Dad tonight. I'll ask him if I can come tomorrow. Okay?"

"Good!" agreed Tomasito.

After giving the briefest possible answers to the questions asked him by Johnnie and Teresa, Tomasito hastened to the corral. Allca and Quilla came to him at once, rubbing against him to show their pleasure at his return. Kuzni and Puca joined them. Tomasito talked to them in Quechua, stroking and patting them.

"Come, my friends," he said at last. "Let us go to the lovely mountain." He opened the gate and directed the llamas toward the steep, rocky slopes to the southwest. They raised their heads higher and strode along with a firm step. They seemed to be rejoicing in a challenge worthy of them. Tomasito finally brought them to a halt and let them graze on the tough, sparse ground cover of a rocky ledge.

Soon it was dark and cold in the shadow of the rock wall, although the sun still burnished the eastern peaks. It was time to go home. The brief outing had refreshed both Tomasito and the llamas. Suddenly he realized he was hungry. He even felt ready to talk about school at the dinner table!

110

Both Teresa and Jack were sympathetic when Tomasito told them how hard it was for him to understand the lessons. Teresa reminded him of how they had struggled to learn Spanish and Jack tried to recall the length of time it had taken him to master a foreign language.

"But tomorrow I must read and write!" protested Tomasito.

"Well, at least we can give you a dictionary," Jack offered. "Teresa, where's that Spanish-English one I gave you?"

Teresa found the dictionary and presently the words he must learn for spelling made sense. He wasn't sure he'd remember them, however. Now for the book, *The Red Pony*. Tomasito looked again at the drawing on the cover. "I want to read this," he thought. He began looking up in the dictionary the words on page one. Some he could not find, some Teresa found for him. But many hid from them both. Jack was watching a ball game on TV and they didn't want to bother him. It was nine o'clock and Tomasito still could not tell what had happened on page one.

"You must go to bed now, my brother," insisted Teresa. "The bus comes so early."

"But what will the teacher say? I have not done my lesson! How can I *ever* do it, my sister?"

Teresa comforted him as best she could but she too was worried.

The next day on the bus Tomasito asked Joe, "Did you read the lesson?"

"No," Joe replied. "I had to help my father load some scrap metal. And after dinner he was watching the ball game, so it was hard to read. It was a good game, though. Did you see it?"

"I was trying to read *The Red Pony*. Too difficult!" replied Tomasito. "What will the teacher say?"

111

"Oh, nothing much. I don't think she knows we're there."

At school they were tested on their reading homework. Tomasito had never seen a test like it. There were ten sentences, with a word left out in each sentence. You had to think of the right word to put in each blank space. Since Tomasito could grasp only dimly the meaning of the sentences and had not read the story anyway, he could not complete the test. In spelling he tried to write all the words. The work was corrected in class. Some of his words were spelled right but most were wrong. Mrs. Hohman did not scold. In fact, she seemed to have something else on her mind.

As the days and weeks went by, school was both better and worse for Tomasito. One day he found, to his astonishment, that he had understood all that the teacher had said. On the other hand, he seldom finished the assigned reading. And English composition baffled him completely. Even when he had really struggled to compose a perfect paper, the teacher would fill the page with red marks or flatly refuse to correct it. But she never scolded, or discussed his problems with him.

It was this terrible uncertainty which troubled Tomasito. Sometimes he believed he was beginning to catch hold of the ideas behind the strange words, especially when the teacher showed the class nature specimens or they did experiments in science. But then new words would appear and the half-grasped ideas would escape altogether. No matter how much he studied, his grades were always bad. He could never find the right words to fit the empty spaces during the reading tests. He seldom put down English words that the teacher could understand. What would come of it all? What would they do with him?

There was no one to whom Tomasito could turn for help.

112

He did not have the courage to ask the teacher. Besides, she seemed only too willing to forget his very presence.

"Mrs. Hohman was teaching when Daddy went to school," Johnnie explained. "I think she's tired of the whole thing. She was going to retire, but Mr. Hohman died and she kept on teaching." Johnnie sometimes tried to help but he wasn't very good at explaining things. Jack, who had not liked school very much himself, had neither the skill nor the patience to help the boy. Teresa was always encouraging and comforting and she had absolute faith that Tomasito would go to the University. But she could not write English either.

Joe continued to get poor grades, which puzzled Tomasito. Joe read the books; he even borrowed some from the book-mobile. But he rarely bothered to do the homework when it was assigned and almost defiantly failed the tests. "Stupid test!" he would say, laughing. "Why should I fill in all those little spaces? Kid games! I know when I know something!"

He was particularly disdainful of history. "I hate history!" he announced. "We read over and over again how the white men invaded America and how they finally killed enough Indians to take over the whole land. Last year I liked reading about the kingdoms of the Incas and the Aztecs. But they were beaten too. Why should I read history?"

Tomasito was silent. He remembered how he had felt in Cuzco when he had realized that the beautiful Golden Enclosure and all the Inca treasures had been destroyed by the Spaniards. He wished he could remember just what Don Pedro had told him so that in turn he could explain to Joe why Indians must study.

He sometimes tried. "Joe, don't you want to learn so you can go to high school and help your country? Don Pedro says our country needs the Indians."

113

"What could I do if I did go to high school? There is no work for Washos. My father went to high school. But when he got out there were no jobs for him. He has a hard time earning a living from his auto wrecking. Some of the Washo men never get a steady job. Why knock myself out?" Tomasito did not know what to answer.

Joe was not much help in school, but he was an expert guide to out-of-school pleasures. Most afternoons, when he did not have to help his father, he would go with Tomasito to pasture the llamas on the mountain.

Joe knew the surrounding mountains by heart and Jack permitted Tomasito to hike with him far up the rocky slopes to lonely meadows or along a mountain stream. On weekends the boys would load their sleeping bags on Allca and Kuzni and spend the night in the open. While the llamas grazed on the highland fodder the boys searched for abandoned mines and Indian camp sites or practiced snaring rabbits. Joe's father would not let him carry a gun but had taught him how to make the clever snares which Washos had depended on long before the white man came.

Joe would sometimes collect pine nuts to surprise his mother and grandmother. "White people make fun of us for eating pine-nut soup," he explained, "but it is good when you are used to it."

It was on one of these trips that Joe took Tomasito to meet his grandmother. She lived in a little house near the clearing. She. was really Joe's great-grandmother and was very very old. "She was a famous Indian doctor when she was younger," Joe said. "Some people call her a witch, but the Indians who knew her in the olden days say she always used her magic to cure people. Now we go to white doctors, but once she was much respected. I guess she's the last Indian doctor left."

114

"In Peru we have Indian doctors, too," said Tomasito. "We say *curandera*."

Granny Henry was so wrinkled and shriveled that all that appeared to be alive were her black eyes, which seemed to pierce the visitor's mind. Joe explained to her in Washo, which was all she spoke, who Tomasito was and then opened her door wide so that she could watch them unload Kuzni. She gazed intently at Tomasito and at Kuzni and nodded her head as if in approval when the sack of pine nuts was laid in her lap.

"I think she liked you," observed Joe afterwards. "She can tell a good person by looking at him. Some people used to be afraid of her eyes. But I think they were bad people. They thought she could see inside them so they said she hexed them."

Tomasito was thankful she had liked him. Tío Dominguez had said that the *curandera* in Pisac had once hexed one of his llamas and made it die.

Joe had become Tomasito's coach in North American games. On clear Sunday afternoons, he would come over to teach him football. Johnnie was glad to join in the game and usually rounded up several friends. The younger boys were proud to practice with a well-known player like Joe. Even Jack and Pat sometimes joined in. Tomasito longed for the day when he would be good enough to play with the big Indian boys over at Joe's.

On Saturdays when it was too stormy to take the llamas to the mountains the men and boys would watch football on TV. Joe was invited to join the McGerraghtys. Tomasito noticed that when Joe had the courage to express his views, they were listened to respectfully by the men.

115

"I hear you're a great baseball player," Pat said one day. "But you're not bad at football either."

"I like baseball best," replied Joe. "I wish we could teach Tommy baseball before spring. But now he needs to know football. I guess he'll catch on."

And so the time out of school became filled with good things—games, mountain hikes, animals, and friends. More and more Tomasito depended on these things to clear his mind of the pain and worry brought about by school. However, one day at the end of October he was brought face to face with his problem.

"Well, guys, be prepared!" announced one of the boys on the homeward-bound school bus. "You know what will be waiting for us when we get home—report cards! They mailed them to our parents yesterday."

Tomasito, who had not anticipated this, was stunned. He somehow managed to climb off the bus at his stop. He went first to the barn, then began to climb the accustomed mountain trail. He thought of hiding in the mountains with the llamas, of never returning, of hiding in one of the old mine shafts and living off rabbits and pine nuts. It had grown quite dark before he had the courage to go home.

Teresa was in the barn looking for him. When she saw him she put her arms around him, crying, "Oh, my brother, I was so worried about you!"

Tomasito did not explain. He went silently into the house with her. On the mantelpiece in the living room he saw an envelope. He sat down before the TV set, rigid with listening for Jack. Eventually, the kitchen door slammed. Tomasito heard Jack greeting Teresa. It seemed an hour before he came in.

116

"Hi, Tommy!" Jack reached for the envelope. "Well, I see the principal has sent your report card."

As Tomasito watched him read the report, he could tell that Jack was shocked. He looked shaken and cleared his throat before he spoke. "Well, kid," he said finally, more in bewilderment than anger. "It's really bad, isn't it! All F's except in Music and Citizenship! *Díos mío!* What shall we do?"

Tomasito could hardly speak. Jack's dismay was harder to bear than a beating.

"I don't know, Señor Jack. I try as hard as I can."

Jack thought for awhile. At last he said, "I'm just not a teacher, Tommy. I can't help you. But I don't think you're stupid. Maybe by the next report period you'll know more English words."

"I'll try, *señor*—"

Tomasito was silent at the dinner table. He scarely ate. After Teresa had washed the dishes she went to him in his room. She found him at his desk, his head on his arms.

"Don't grieve, my brother," she comforted. "You will learn in time. I know how smart you are. Don Pedro knew it too."

The mention of Don Pedro brought tears to Tomasito's eyes. "No, I cannot do those tests. I cannot write English. I have tried as hard as I can. Now I can never go home. Papá and Don Pedro would be ashamed of me. And Jack is ashamed of me here."

Teresa did her best to console him but he would not be comforted. At last she gave up and left him to think things out for himself.

117

Winter

THE trees in the canyon bottoms, full of red and yellow leaves in the fall, were now skeleton-like in their bareness. Winter had come and storms of wind and rain kept the boys inside on weekends. At last it began to snow. The first snowfalls did not prevent Tomasito from taking the llamas up the mountain. There were still sheltered places where they could find food and their cleated hooves kept them secure on the icy trails. But little by little, as snow was added to snow, it became impossible for the animals to locate fodder. Tomasito could see now why Jack had insisted that hay must be provided for winter and he gloated over a loft filled with the fragrant stuff. What a joy it was each morning to toss down forkfuls of the dried grass he and his friends had cut from the summer meadow!

"What will you do now for hard food?" asked Joe one day. "You said the llamas had to keep grinding off their teeth."

"I don't know," replied Tomasito. "I must think of something. The llamas might eat carrots and corncobs. Especially the corncobs. But where would I get them?"

"Mr. Sorenson sometimes has leftover carrots he gives away for pets," suggested Joe. "I don't know if any of the ranchers still have any corncobs. Why don't we walk into town and talk to Mr. Sorenson?"

"Okay," agreed Tomasito. "I will take the llamas so they can get some exercise."

The afternoon sun glistened on the snow which the plows had piled high on either side of the highway. The llamas picked their way along on the scraped surface, red tassels bobbing and Allca's bells tinkling in the winter air.

"Just like a Christmas card!" exclaimed Mrs. Sorenson, who had been watching their approach from the door. "To be sure, I never heard of Santa using llamas, but it might be a good idea! Say, Tommy, do you suppose we could use your llamas in the Christmas pageant?"

She went on to explain to Tomasito that the community always had a tree-lighting ceremony in front of the old primary school at Christmastime. Sometimes they had a Santa Claus, but this year they were planning to have a pageant showing the manger and the shepherds and Wise Men bringing gifts to the Christ Child.

"It would almost be like having real camels." Mrs. Sorenson's enthusiasm was growing as she told them about it. "You and Joe and another of the big boys could be Wise Men."

Tomasito was a little frightened at the idea of appearing in public. Joe was hesitant, too. On the other hand, they could see that this would be quite an honor. The boys agreed to think the matter over.

They then broached the subject of tooth-grinding foods to Mr. Sorenson. "I think corncobs would be best," he said. "I don't know if any of the ranchers still have any. I'll inquire around and see how much they would cost. In the meantime, you may try out these carrots to see if the animals like them." The boys thanked him.

"Don't forget to ask your folks about the Christmas pageant," Mrs. Sorenson called after them.

On the way home the boys discussed the pageant. "I might feel funny, dressed like a king," worried Tomasito.

"I would, too," agreed Joe.

"But it would be an honor for the llamas to serve the Child Jesus. He might like to have them bring the presents."

"Maybe I wouldn't feel like a sissy if I could be with the llamas," speculated Joe. "Do you think we could get Sandy to be the other king?"

Jack encouraged Tomasito to be in the pageant and Mr. Henry consented to Joe's participation. Sandy was finally prevailed upon to join them, provided it would look as though he were driving Kuzni. Eventually, it turned out that the McGerraghty household was asked to make quite a contribution to the event, for Teresa was to be Mary and was to ride to the manger on one of the burros.

The Christmas season made Tomasito and Teresa very homesick. They thought of Papá and Domitila and the children. They wondered daily if the small Christmas presents they had mailed in November had made the long trip successfully.

One day Teresa found a letter in the mailbox, postmarked Cuzco. There was also a card for Tomasito. The letter was from Domitila. Everyone was well, she wrote. The government had begun to send special tourist buses out from Cuzco and Papá had been busy as a guide. Pablo had applied for a job driving one of the buses and they thought he would begin work around Christmas. They were all going to Pisac for the holidays if the government would give them leave.

Teresa wept. Tomasito stared at the card addressed to him. It was from Don Pedro. "How is my new scholar?" it read. "New diggings are opening up all over Peru, so we will need you. Best wishes for the New Year. Pedro Guzman-Barrera."

Tomasito turned quite pale. "Pray for me, my sister. I could not bear to disappoint Don Pedro."

The Christmas pageant was truly a welcome diversion. School was out by the middle of December and the children and some of their parents had time to build the manger and to rehearse. The primary-school children were to dress as angels and sing carols, so Sharon rehearsed too. She was very pleased. "But I wish they would let Quilla be in the play. She is so pretty," she remarked one day.

"But Sharon, you know there were only three Wise Men," objected Johnnie.

"Well, why couldn't they put Quilla in the stable with the burro?"

"Say, that's a pretty good idea, isn't it, Tommy?" Johnnie broke in. "Would Quilla stay in the stable?"

"Yes, she'd stay with Teresa."

"Then I'll ask Mrs. Sorenson." And off Johnnie went. Mrs. Sorenson agreed at once.

On Christmas Eve Jack and Pat came home early. Both families hurried through dinner so that the boys could start to town with the animals. Joe came to help with the burro. Tomasito had curried the llamas until their fur gleamed like silk. Teresa had made new red wool tassels to decorate their ears and Allca's bells had been polished till they caught the light like jewels.

By the time the boys arrived at the schoolhouse, most of

121

the other performers were on hand. The Highway Department snowplows had carved a huge semicircle in the snow opposite the old building so that the audience could stand, or be seated on folding chairs, protected from the wind by walls of snow. In front of the school grew a huge pine, a perfect green cone, which had been used for many years as the town Christmas tree.

Tonight, beneath the tree stood the stable at Bethlehem, a wooden shelter which contained the traditional manger. Tomasito could see Mrs. Sorenson arranging the figure of the Baby Jesus. The primary-school children, in angel robes, were chasing each other with snowballs, evading parents who were trying to line them up on the other side of the tree. Joe delivered the burro to Mrs. Sorenson, who had the good sense to tie it securely to the schoolhouse porch. Tomasito lined up the llamas behind the stable.

At the last minute it was learned that Joseph had had a flat tire and Mr. Sorenson was sent to his rescue. Two shepherds absent-mindedly let go of their lambs and they were promptly chased by a dog which had escaped from somebody's car. At last, however, everything seemed to settle into place. The audience, wrapped in blankets, waited quietly. The night was clear and the wind moved softly through the great Christmas tree.

The voices of the children began "O Little Town of Bethlehem." There was Joseph and there was Mary—Teresa in her Quechuan dress with her winter shawl over her head, riding on the burro. The innkeeper came out to meet them, shook his head, and pointed to the stable. The children sang "Away In A Manger."

Suddenly the lights went on in the stable. Tomasito, watching from the sidelines, drew in his breath. Teresa, her beautiful oval face bent over the manger, looked just like the statue of the Holy Mother he had seen in church. Beside the manger stood the little burro and at her side, legs folded primly beneath her, lay the white llama, Quilla.

"Quilla is like a Holy Mother for the animals," Tomasito thought.

The shepherds entered, the angels moved closer to look at the Child, and the children began "We Three Kings Of Orient Are."

"Come, Tommy," whispered Joe. "That's our cue." Tomasito, now alert, whistled gently to the llamas. Joe and Allca went first, then Sandy with Kuzni, and finally Tomasito and Puca. Their tall crowns gleamed in the light. The solemn music paced the swaying gait of the llamas. As Allca reached the stable Tomasito signalled to him to stop, but Allca did a strange thing. Without command, he quietly folded his legs beneath him as if he too would kneel before the Holy Child.

"O Come All Ye Faithful," sang the children, and the audience joined in.

After the lights had been turned out in the stable, the players joined the audience to admire the Christmas tree.

"Could you help with the presents?" Mr. Sorenson asked Tomasito.

Mr. Buffer, the mayor of the city as well as the manager of the Sierra Motel, was speaking to the audience. "And now, my friends, if you will stay in your places, there will be presents for the children. Tonight Santa Claus was very busy, so he asked the Three Kings to help us out."

Tomasito guided Puca and Johnnie proudly directed Kuzni up and down the rows of people, while Joe and Sandy gave little bags of candy from the packs on the llamas' backs to each child. It was a rare child who did not pat the soft fur and say, "Merry Christmas, llama! Merry Christmas, Tommy!" as they passed.

Mr. Sorenson volunteered to take the llamas and burro home in his truck. Before he and Joe separated, Tomasito shyly thrust a little package into his friend's pocket. "Teresa made it for you. Merry Christmas!"

"My mother made something for you, too," laughed Joe. "I left it under your tree. Merry Christmas!"

When the family got home, Teresa made hot chocolate and they sat drinking it before the fireplace, admiring their own lighted Christmas tree and thinking of the beautiful evening. Tomasito noticed that there was something very special about the way Jack looked at his lovely young wife. Tomasito and Teresa spoke of how far away from home they had felt the day before. "But now we all seem closer," observed Tomasito.

"Yes," agreed Teresa, "Christmas is everywhere!"

The day after Christmas, Tomasito, Joe, and the llama set off for Mr. Sorenson's to see him about the corncobs. Allca was carrying a pair of saddle baskets which Mrs. Henry had made as Joe's Christmas present to Tomasito. They were like two Washo cradles without canopies. Joe walked along, proudly wearing the Peruvian cap which Teresa had woven for him.

They found Mr. Sorenson unexpectedly busy. The early snowfall had brought skiers to the newly opened resort. The store was full of tourists in ski outfits, buying sun-tan lotion and candy bars, asking the way to the resort, and calling on Mr. Sorenson to pump gasoline. It was clear to the boys that nobody in the store would have time to discuss llama fodder for some time. Tomasito decided to buy a bunch of carrots for the llamas and a candy bar to share with Joe.

124

In the meantime, the llamas, lined up along the snowbank outside, were creating quite a sensation.

"Aren't they cute!" Tomasito heard somebody squeal as the door opened.

"I wish I could ride one," said a child.

When Tomasito and Joe returned to the llamas, Mr. Sorenson was pumping gas. "You ought to have winter llama rides, Tommy. The tourists are crazy about those animals."

"I wish I could," agreed Tomasito. "Then I could buy some corncobs for them."

At dinner the next evening Jack said, "Tommy, Mr. Gardner, who owns the new ski resort, has some business to discuss with you. Pat and I were finishing the work on the ski lift today and Gardner asked if maybe they could have llama rides at the resort. What do you think?"

"Maybe without the rig?" Tomasito suggested.

"You can ride over with us tomorrow and talk to him about it."

"How could we manage the rides without the turntable, Tommy?" asked Mr. Gardner, the next day.

"Three children ride down the hill and up again. Or maybe ski lift for children?"

"Say! That's a good idea!" agreed Mr. Gardner. "The little children who go sliding on the baby slope could ride a llama up for a quarter! Of course you'd have to pull up the sled or the skis."

"Our burro could pull them," Tomasito nodded. "My friend Joe could drive the burro."

"Very good! I would be willing to let you have all the profit. The llamas will make the resort more attractive. A lot of people noticed them at Sorenson's."

So it was agreed. Every Saturday and Sunday during the

125

skiing season, when the weather was good, Tomasito would bring his llamas to Gardner's Resort.

The llamas made a pretty sight with their red tassels and laughing riders. Many families said they would come to ski at Gardner's again because the little children had such fun. Many pictures were taken. Tomasito and Joe were often included as, in their Peruvian caps, they looked very picturesque. One of the tourists gave Tomasito a snapshot to send home to Peru. He proudly sent it to Papá, together with a copy of the *Muir County Herald* which had printed pictures of the Christmas pageant.

Tomasito found that he had no trouble speaking English to the tourists at the ski resort. They reminded him of the passengers on the ship coming from Peru. "Margit would be surprised if she could hear me," he thought.

Tomasito had learned to speak English, but the semester report card, which arrived a few days later, did not show much progress. Jack and Teresa looked at the list of grades.

"Good, Tommy," cheered his sister. "You did much better in mathematics."

"Yes," agreed Jack. "A C in math is a lot better than an F. But what are we going to do if you keep on getting D's and F's in most of the other subjects? The school might not let you pass into the eighth grade."

Tomasito felt terror.

"Maybe Aunt Kathy could help you some, Tommy," said Jack presently. "She used to be a schoolteacher. I'll ask her if she can help you a couple of nights a week."

Aunt Kathy did start to help him. One evening she came over to the old house, gave Tomasito some practice in spelling, and showed him how to begin writing a report. He began

126

to feel a little hope. But Aunt Kathy had many responsibilities and their sessions after that often had to be cancelled.

Then, one stormy night in late February, Teresa's son was born.

Jack had to drive through the storm to South Tahoe for the doctor as the telephone lines were down. The baby was born early in the morning. He was called Paul, after Teresa's brother Pablo.

After that, the household seemed to revolve around Baby Paul. Aunt Kathy took care of Teresa and provided meals for Jack and Tomasito. Jack thought of no one but his wife and son. The evening lessons were forgotten and Tomasito was left to struggle on alone. He felt deserted. Night after night, he went out to the barn to put his arms around Quilla and to whisper, "Soon you will have a baby, too. But you won't make such a silly fuss about it—like people."

The Broken Idol

IT WAS a rough spring and there was snow until Easter. The skiers kept coming to Gardner's whenever they could get through the pass. The Highway Department did its best to keep the pass open but sometimes blizzards during the night would wipe out the work of the day before. Mr. Gardner could never tell when the resort would be full and Tomasito and Joe never knew when they would have llama riders. Most of the time, Pat and Jack were able to get down to Tahoe to work. But sometimes they too were kept at home by the storms. Even the school buses could not move.

Everybody became weary of the long winter. Even the spring rains were welcome, until the old-timers began saying, "Too much rain. The snow is melting too fast. There won't be enough snow pack for the summer. And there will be floods!"

The floods arrived as predicted, bringing misery to Parson's Flat. As the river rose higher, the Indian homes along its banks were endangered. Tents were erected on the bluffs and cots were laid out in the old schoolhouse and in the town hall. Stricken families, lugging bundles up the slippery trail in the pouring rain, had salvaged only what they could carry.

Urgent appeals were sent to the governor. The Red Cross finally brought in food and clothing.

The *Muir County Herald* printed an editorial which read, "The Bureau of Public Works will not acknowledge responsibility for flood control on the Wilson River ... How many times will this happen again?"

One damp, cold morning Tomasito went as usual to care for the llamas before going to school. He slipped and sloshed through the icy mud to the barn. He climbed first to the loft and tossed down a forkful of hay to each animal. Then, as was his custom, he went to pet and stroke and talk to them. The male llamas responded as usual, then began to eat. But Quilla! What was the matter? It was too soon for her kid to be born. She must be sick. She did not stand up to greet him and paid no attention to the fresh hay. Tomasito knelt down beside her and felt her all over. Her ears and muzzle were hot, her mouth dry, and her eyes glazed. As he stroked her, she suddenly fell over on her side and remained motionless and limp.

He rushed to the water pail, dipped in his handkerchief, and moistened the animal's parched lips. Then he ran to the house to tell Teresa. Teresa was feeding her baby. Jack had already gone to work.

"Go quickly to Aunt Kathy's. Johnnie will tell Myrtle your llama is sick and you cannot go to school. Perhaps Aunt Kathy will help us."

Aunt Kathy came over with Timmy after Johnnie and Sharon had gone to school. "Will you stay here with the baby while I go to the barn?" asked Teresa.

"Perhaps you should not go near the sick animal, Teresa,

with such a young baby. It may have an infection that is catching. I'll go with Tommy and see if I can think of something. Timmy can stay with you."

When Aunt Kathy saw the weak and feverish animal, she shook her head. "The poor thing! It must have an awful temperature! I don't know much about animals. With children you'd try to get the fever down. I'm sure it's an infection. Let me see if I can get hold of a vet by telephone."

Aunt Kathy tried all morning to reach a veterinarian, but telephone wires were down in many places. She finally reached the home of one doctor, who had gone out to try to save a sick horse. His wife had no idea when he'd return but she would have him call back when he did.

Tomasito sat with Quilla all day. He bathed her head and belly and tried to pour some water into her mouth. At the same time, he tried to keep out the gusty drafts which were threatening to burst through the door. But Quilla lay limp, her eyes closed, not moving at all. It seemed to Tomasito as though time stood completely still. Finally Teresa came to the barn door with a jar of soup and some crackers for his lunch. "Poor little creature!" she mourned. "And so soon she will have her kid. But do not lose hope, my brother. Llamas are very strong and perhaps the animal doctor will call before long."

The afternoon passed slowly and it began to get dark. Tomasito was thinking of turning on the barn light when a car drove up close to the door. It was Joe Henry and his father. Joe carried a thermos bottle.

"Johnnie told us about Quilla," he said. "And when I got home I told Granny. She got out some old pieces of bark she had and made this tea. She said it is very good for fevers."

"I don't know if you want to try it or not," Mr. Henry

130

added. "It won't hurt our feelings if you don't. But they say that in the old days Granny was a good doctor."

Tomasito was so grateful for his friends' help that he could not find words to thank them. At the same time, he did not quite know what to do. He could not help but remember Tío Dominguez' story of the *curandera* of Pisac. Besides, Quilla really belonged to Jack. Tomasito explained the latter problem to the Henrys.

"Perhaps you should wait till Jack comes home," suggested Mr. Henry. "The tea will keep warm in the thermos."

Fortunately, Jack came soon. He too shook his head as he looked at Quilla. "I tried to get the vet again," he reported. "But his wife was afraid he might not get back tonight. As far as I can see, the poor thing couldn't be worse off than she is now and the tea just might help. I know my father used to set quite a bit of store by Granny's medicines."

So Tomasito held the llama's mouth open while Sam poured in the liquid. It was hard to get Quilla to swallow but Jack massaged her throat until she did.

"The only other thing I can suggest might be some sulfa tablets they gave us in the Navy," Jack said presently. "I don't see how they could interfere with the tea and they might help out with the infection."

They got Quilla to swallow two of the tablets.

"Now all we can do is wait, I guess," Jack sighed. "Tommy, I'll stay with Quilla while you have some supper. Won't you and Joe eat with us, Sam?"

"No, thanks, my wife is waiting for us."

"Could I stay with Tommy?" Joe asked his father.

"Please let him," begged Tomasito.

"You might not get much sleep, but I know it would mean a lot to Tommy," Jack said.

131

"Well, all right," consented Mr. Henry. "Maybe the two of you could take turns watching and both get a little sleep that way."

"Thanks, Sam," Jack nodded. "You boys have supper, then bring two sleeping bags out with you when you come back. I'll stay till you come. One of you can call me in the night if there's any trouble."

Of course nobody could tell whether it was Granny's tea or the sulfa pills, or both, which did the good work. But Quilla did recover from the fever. However, her kid was born dead a few days later. Tomasito was so relieved that Quilla had been spared he could only partially mourn the loss of the baby.

"The zoo will have to wait another year for its new llama. I hope Quilla won't be sick again."

Jack said he thought the change of hemispheres had had a lot to do with Quilla's illness. "If we had been in Peru, it would have been summer," he reminded Tomasito. "I think she'll get used to the different seasons soon."

Quilla was Granny Henry's last cure. Shortly after the llama's recovery, Tomasito reported that Joe had been absent from school for two days.

"Yes," said Uncle Pat. "Granny Henry passed away. Her descendants and relations have come from all the Washo communities to attend her funeral. Even Sam's brother, Joe, has come from the university at Berkeley. But, Tommy, don't ask Joe about Granny. The Washos don't ever mention a person who has died. They think if they do, the spirit must return from the land of the dead."

Tomasito mourned Granny. He wished he could have thanked her for having helped Quilla.

Joe finally returned to school. "My Uncle Joe is here for

awhile," he told Tomasito. "Could you come to our house after school? He'd like to meet you."

Uncle Joe was helping Sam Henry dismantle a car when the boys got off the bus that afternoon. He stopped work and came forward when he saw them coming. "So this is Tommy!" he said.

From his warm smile and friendly voice, Tomasito felt that Uncle Joe already knew him and had decided to be his friend. Uncle Joe must be a lot younger than his brother Sam, Tomasito thought. It was not so much his face as his manner that made him feel this. Uncle Joe did not seem weary; there was no tinge of bitterness in his voice. Listening to him talk made Tomasito feel about the world as he had felt about the wild hay in the meadow—that thought and skill and hard work would bring things to harvest in spite of obstacles.

Uncle Joe had special news. "Now that I have passed my bar exam and am a lawyer I want to use my education to help my people. Elections are coming up soon and I've decided to run for public office."

"What does that mean, sir?" inquired Tomasito.

"That means I am going to try to get the people to elect me Supervisor of this county.

"Do you think they will elect you, Uncle Joe?" asked his nephew. "There has never been an Indian Supervisor, has there?"

"No," replied Uncle Joe. "But no Washo has tried to be elected. That's the trouble with us here, Tomasito. We feel we have suffered injustices, but we don't try to fight for our rights."

"How does a person get elected?" asked Joe.

"Well, that's where I need your help. I have some handbills, telling the voters who I am and what I would like to do if

133

elected. Will you boys help me take them around to the people?"

The boys were delighted. "But I will have to get permission from Jack," Tomasito said.

Jack was a little hesitant at first about letting Tomasito take part in this campaign. "What do I know about Joe Henry? He was just a little kid when I went into the Navy." Jack was about to say something about Indians in politics when his glance rested on little Paul, sitting on his Indian mother's lap. So he said instead, "What makes you think he will be a good Supervisor, Tommy?"

"Oh, he's very smart. He's been to the university. He's a lawyer. My friend says Uncle Joe is the first Washo lawyer in Muir County."

"That may be," argued Jack. "But being smart is not enough. We wouldn't want a smart Supervisor who was no good."

"Uncle Joe says he will try to get flood control for the river so the houses won't be hurt again. He will get more park and resort jobs too. That would help you, would it not, Jack?"

Jack laughed. "You're a pretty smart campaigner, Tommy. Maybe Uncle Joe will win after all. Okay. You go with your friend. It will be a good education for you. But don't forget to keep up that school work!"

Jack was right. Tomasito did learn a lot—about people, about Indians, about the United States. Uncle Joe was a hero to Tomasito and Joe. As they listened to his campaign speeches they thought he spoke truths which no one could resist. Everybody must surely vote for Uncle Joe! But when they took his campaign literature around they found many people who would not even read it.

Some said, "Thinks he's smart, doesn't he, now that he's been to college!" Or, "I don't trust lawyers, especially an

Indian lawyer!" Or, "What could a Washo do if he did get elected? He wouldn't stand a chance against those politicians!"

Of course there were some who were as eager as the boys for Uncle Joe to win. One of them was the new eighth-grade teacher, Miss Ramirez. Joe and Tomasito handed her a handbill as she was going to her car one day after school. She read it at once and asked the boys questions about Uncle Joe and what he expected to do for Muir County. Miss Ramirez was quite young and pretty. The boys had to think fast to answer her questions.

"Good, boys," she said at last. "You have given me some fine reasons for voting for Mr. Henry. If you'll let me have some of that literature, I'll pass it out to my friends." She closed the car door and smiled at them through the window. "By the way, Joe and Tommy, after all this, I'm expecting you to get an A in eighth-grade social studies!"

Joe and Tomasito looked at each other a little sheepishly after she had left. "I wish I had worked harder," admitted Joe. "Suppose they won't let us go on to eighth grade? Then we'd have to stay another year with Mrs. Hohman instead of having Miss Ramirez!"

Tomasito's face fell. "My last report card was a little better, but it's so hard to study! I don't even feel like doing it. I don't think I can do any better. I wish we had had Miss Ramirez this year!"

The next day Uncle Joe came to pick up the boys after school so that they could take some election literature over to Ashford.

"Miss Ramirez said she would give handbills to her friends," reminded young Joe. "Let's take her some right away."

135

Uncle Joe gave them a packet of flyers and went with them to meet Miss Ramirez. He thanked her for her interest and they talked a long time about all the improvements that should be made in the county.

The boys, bored with being ignored, went over to the baseball diamond. Tomasito practiced batting. He had learned a lot from Joe and Johnnie about baseball. "Maybe next year I can really play with Joe," he thought.

Later, on the trip to Ashford, Uncle Joe talked to the boys about school.

"You really think you might not pass?" he asked after they had recounted their difficulties. "You mean you'd have to stay another year with old Mrs. Hohman instead of having Miss Ramirez? I'd hate to miss a chance to have her for a teacher myself!"

More seriously, he went on to question the boys about their work and why they were getting such poor grades. He told them some of the reasons why Indian boys in particular should work hard in school. "We're now getting a chance to show people what a good job Indians can do. But how can we, if we aren't educated? It's the same in Peru, isn't it, Tommy? Quechuan boys can become good archeologists but they have to go to the University."

"But I just want to play baseball," objected young Joe.

"You need to go to high school to even become a good ball player in this country."

Young Joe didn't understand this very well, but if Uncle Joe said he should study, then study he must.

"But I *try* to study and I can't learn," complained Tomasito.

"It's hard, I know," agreed Uncle Joe. "But since you boys have helped me, I will help you. Every evening I will work

136

with you an hour on your homework. Beginning tomorrow. Okay, Tommy?"

Every evening after that, Uncle Joe worked with the boys. Uncle Joe made everything seem interesting. He told them stories that made them proud to be Indians. He invented math problems based on the economics of the llama rides. He helped Tomasito with his written English. The boys worked harder and they began to get better grades on their papers.

But Mrs. Hohman continued to hand their work back without comment. It was almost June now and the boys found it impossible to learn everything they had not mastered earlier.

One day the fatal message came. A note from the principal's office asked Jack to meet with Mr. Thomas and Mrs. Hohman. During the interview they told him that they felt sure Tomasito should not go on to eighth grade.

"He has handed in surprisingly better papers lately, I see," admitted Mr. Thomas. "But Mrs. Hohman thinks he hasn't the background for eighth-grade work. I'm very sorry, Mr. McGerraghty."

Jack didn't know what to say to the principal. And it would be harder still to announce the bad news to Tomasito himself. He asked Teresa to help him and together they told the boy what Mr. Thomas had said. Teresa put her arms around her brother, tried to say things to give him hope and to make him look into the distant future. But Tomasito felt as if a light had been extinguished inside him.

When it was time for the bus the next day (there was a week of school left), Tomasito could not be found. Later, Teresa saw that the llamas had been driven from the barn.

137

Wretchedly, she watched for them to come back. What if Tomasito should run away into the mountains?

At the end of the day Tomasito returned. Nothing was said. The boy felt himself go through all the expected motions—dinner, bed, school the next morning—but mechanically, as if somehow his spirit had left his body to perform like a wound-up toy.

Sitting next to Joe on the school bus, Tomasito forced himself to look at his friend's face. In it he saw a reflection of his own mood, accented by the bitter disdain which Joe had displayed last summer. Later, Joe told him that he too was not going to pass.

"See? What did I tell you!" he sneered.

After school that afternoon Tomasito went to his room, to find Teresa seated at his desk. Her head was buried in her arms and she was sobbing. Hearing him come in, she raised her head and held out her hand. In it were the fragments of the clay llama Don Pedro had given him. Teresa had shown it to Baby Paul, she told him. Reaching out to it, the baby had knocked it from her hand to the floor.

Tomasito said nothing. Silently, he took the broken pieces from her hand and put them away in his desk. Then he walked from the room.

He went to the barn and lay down beside Allca on the straw. "*Ay!*" Allca, my brother," he sobbed, pushing his face into the rough fur. "Why did I ever come to California? This infant Paul will be the ruin of me. First he separated me from my sister and robbed me of the help I needed. And now he has destroyed Don Pedro's talisman, my good luck charm. He is nothing but a North American demon. I hate him!"

The next Tuesday was election day. At breakfast Jack said, "Today we vote, Tommy. I am going to vote for Joe Henry.

138

You boys really sold me on him. I don't know if he'll win, but he's put up a good fight."

Tomasito tried to smile as he answered, "I'm glad, Jack." But somehow his crippled spirit could not muster even enough hope to concern itself with his hero's fate.

That evening, however, he did stay in the living room instead of going to his own room as was his custom lately. The polls closed at seven o'clock. Muir County was so small that by nine o'clock all of the votes had been counted. Of the three-hundred-fifty votes cast, only thirty were for Uncle Joe.

"I can't understand it!" exclaimed Jack. "I thought he'd have a hard time winning against old Mattson. After all, Mattson had been Supervisor for twenty years. But thirty votes! Why, there must be at least a hundred Indian voters!"

Tomasito could hardly bear this final blow. His past, his future, and now his hero—all had been destroyed.

The Pieces of the Past

"Has your Uncle Joe gone away again?" Tomasito asked Joe one day, as the boys sat in the shade of the pine trees waiting for a second summer of llama rides to begin. The turnstile was set up in its old location and the animals were waiting patiently in their places. This time, Tomasito was not so worried about lack of customers. It was not yet the Fourth of July so he did not really expect very many people today.

"No," replied Joe, looking up from the *Muir County Herald*. "Uncle Joe's still here. He may go to Sacramento in a few days to work there till fall. But he says he wants to find out first why he got so few votes in the election. He's going to come back and run for office again."

"Again!" exclaimed Tomasito. "But suppose he loses again?"

"He might have to try many times in many elections," returned Joe. "He says it's so important for the Washos to

140

have a Supervisor who will help them that he must keep on trying."

"Look here!" Joe continued, pointing to the newspaper. "The editor of the *Herald* talks about Uncle Joe. He says, 'Perhaps if Mr. Joe Henry had returned to Muir County earlier, he might have made a better showing. He should have gotten to know personally every voter in the district. He should have made the Indian community feel that he was still one of them and not a smart lawyer from the city, trying to put something over on them.' Maybe the editor is right."

Just then a carload of young children celebrating a birthday stopped near the turnstile and the boys had to interrupt their conversation. But, as he walked around with Allca, Tomasito kept thinking of how hard it would be for Uncle Joe to try again to be elected. How would he be brave enough to plead with all those voters who had turned him down before?

A few evenings later, Tomasito was cleaning out the llama stalls. As was so often the case now, he worked listlessly. The thoughts in his mind turned around and around tiresomely, never getting anywhere. He wished he could go home to Peru. But even if he could go home, he would not be able to endure it because he had disgraced Papá and Don Pedro. He had to stay. But if he had to go back to Mrs. Hohman's class he might not learn any more than last year. Perhaps he would never get into eighth grade. Then Jack would have to send him back to Peru—and that he could not stand!

"Tommy, come up to the house. Uncle Joe has come to see you!" It was Joe, calling to him from the barn door. Tomasito put down his pitchfork.

"Uncle Joe? To see me?"

"Yes, and Miss Ramirez too. They have an idea for us. Come quick!"

141

Tomasito stopped in the kitchen to wash his hands and slick down his hair. He could hear the voices of Uncle Joe and Miss Ramirez. They were talking with Jack in the living room. At last he gathered the courage to join them.

After greetings were over, Jack said, "Tommy, Miss Ramirez has offered to help you and Joe get into eighth grade. Do you boys want to try?"

Tomasito was so astonished that he forgot his English and cried, *"Pues sí, señor!"*

Everybody laughed and Miss Ramirez said "Good! But you boys will really have to keep your noses to the grindstone. I will work with you Monday nights, but every other evening except Sunday you must study for two hours. No baseball! Are you willing?"

Joe hesitated. No baseball! How could he give it up? But Uncle Joe had said he was smart and should go on to high school. Then perhaps he could play with South Tahoe or maybe someday even be picked by one of the professional teams. The Washos would be proud. Of course Uncle Joe thought he should go to college, but four years of high school seemed long enough. Yes, he did want to go to high school. And certainly, if he *had* to go to school, it would be good to be in Miss Ramirez' class. So Joe answered, "Yes, Miss Ramirez, I'll study."

"I'm going to study too," declared Uncle Joe. "Miss Ramirez is going to teach me how to teach the voters to vote for me. Getting elected, you know, will be harder than getting into eighth grade!"

They all laughed and then Miss Ramirez said, as she got up to leave, "Tommy, Teresa says I may use her kitchen as a classroom. So I'll see you boys here next Monday at seven-thirty sharp."

The lessons proved to be a surprise to the boys. Instead of going back to the seventh-grade books, Miss Ramirez made them start right away on eighth-grade work.

"Of course you can do it!" she declared. "But as we go along, I will show you what you need to catch up on from seventh grade. Then we can go back and fill in the gaps."

The boys worked hard. But the first week they were very clumsy at studying. They tried to study together, but they felt embarrassed even with each other. However, they did manage to answer the questions Miss Ramirez gave them concerning the Constitution of the United States. This was an eighth-grade subject. It was true—they *could* do some eighth-grade work! But some of the mathematics problems they couldn't get right at all. And how quickly the time passed! The evenings were over before they had even halfway finished. They were very discouraged.

"It's no use, Miss Ramirez," lamented Joe. "We just can't go as fast as the others. We aren't good enough for eighth grade."

"Nonsense! Is that what you'd say, Joe, if you had to play a tough team in baseball? Of course not! You just need practice. Could you ever hit a home run without practicing? I'm going to show you boys how to study and how to teach each other."

She had them practice reading to themselves, showed them how to track down answers to questions, how to quiz each other, and how to help the other in the subject in which each was best. Tomasito was really good in math, when he understood the problem, and Joe could help him write English that made sense.

"Write, write, write—and read, read, read!" insisted Miss

143

Ramirez. She gave them a schedule of things to do that looked as if it would take a year to accomplish.

But the next week they did considerably better.

"What a lot you have done, boys!" praised their teacher at the end of the session, even though they hadn't quite finished the assignment. Tomasito and Joe were so proud they were speechless.

Study seemed easier each week, but Miss Ramirez pushed them steadily. "Now that you know that you can do the eighth-grade work," she announced one evening, "we'll leave these books, so you won't be bored with them next fall. We'll do some other things instead. Maybe even high school students would like to do these." And she gave them math problems that were like intricate puzzles.

One Sunday the boys made a trip with Jack and Teresa and little Paul to the old Washo campground near Lake Tahoe. Miss Ramirez had made them promise not to read the Forest Service information charts as they went along, but to try and reconstruct the Indian life from what they could see and imagine.

"Let's see how good an archeologist you are, Tommy," Miss Ramirez had challenged him.

Walking up the gentle slope to the comfortable flat where the Washos had camped in the old days was not at all like any expedition on which Tomasito had accompanied Don Pedro. Instead of great cliffs of fitted stone perched on bare precipices, he found a stretch of furry greenery sloping down to the intense blueness of Lake Tahoe.

"I can see why the Washos would want to camp here," he remarked to Joe, "but I can't see anything that has to do with archeology."

"Well, the Washos didn't use many things that would last,"

144

agreed Joe. "But Miss Ramirez did say we might find some-thing of stone."

The boys wandered around happily while Jack and Teresa took little Paul to watch the sparkling rapids of Taylor Creek.

"Say, Joe, do you think this might be what Miss Ramirez meant?" Tomasito called suddenly. He pointed to a large rock, pocked-marked with remarkably smooth, rounded depres-sions. In each depression was a large egg-shaped stone which fitted it exactly. "I don't see how this could be natural. Do you suppose it was a *metate* for corn?"

"You mean a mortar?" asked Joe. "The Washos didn't grind corn but they did grind pine nuts. Maybe that's what it was for. Now we can look at the Forest Service bulletins and see if you were right."

Tomasito was elated to find that his guess had been cor-rect. But the rest of Miss Ramirez' assignment was not so easy. Archeology *was* difficult without stones! The boys sat for a long time with their backs against a pine tree and tried to imagine what it would have been like to live on the Washo campground. Of course Joe had an advantage because Granny Henry had told him stories of the old days.

"Too bad we can't dig around for obsidian knives and things like that," said Joe presently. "But that would be against the law in the National Forest."

But the boys did reconstruct quite a good picture of how it must have been to hunt deer, fish trout from the creek, and eat pine-nut soup by a fragrant campfire.

"I guess I was made for that kind of life instead of school," sighed Joe.

At any rate, their discovery of the mortar stone and their enthusiastic account of life on Taylor Creek pleased Miss Ramirez when they met for lessons on Monday evening.

"Archeology is harder to pursue in California than in Peru," she admitted, "but it will do you good to practice a little, Tomasito."

Finally, there were new books, special ones for each boy. For Joe, the life of Lou Gehrig, for Tomasito a real surprise—the English translation of *The Incas*.

"The book Don Pedro gave me!" exclaimed Tomasito. He blushed when he told Miss Ramirez that he had not even begun to read it.

"Perhaps that's just as well, Tommy. The Spanish might have interfered with your learning English. But now you can write to Don Pedro and tell him that you are becoming a good scholar and writer, like the author, the young Cieza de Léon. He started writing this book, you know, when he was only nineteen!"

That night Tomasito began the English translation. He could hardly stop reading and his light burned far into the night. The next day, as he walked beside the llamas, he imagined himself traveling the Royal Road of the Emperor and visiting the fortresses and cities which Cieza de Léon had described. Now there was no doubt in his mind that he must succeed in the eighth grade and go on to high school.

Joe was learning to study, too. In his case, it was more a matter of training himself, as Miss Ramirez said, instead of passing the time with more pleasant affairs. Miss Ramirez praised him when he began to gain skill in mathematics.

"Now," she told him, "you are exercising your mind just as you are used to exercising your muscles. See how it is beginning to work!"

But one Saturday evening Tomasito waited in vain for Joe to appear for their study session. Since Joe had been in very good health earlier in the day, Tomasito felt sure he could not

146

be sick. Suddenly the boy became aware of what Uncle Pat, who had just come in the door, was saying to Jack. "Thought I'd come over and watch the game with you, Jack, so the kids won't bother me."

Of course! Tonight was that important game that might break the tie between the Giants and the Dodgers. Surely Joe had not been able to resist watching!

Tomasito looked anxiously at the kitchen clock and at Teresa, who was working with her back toward him. He didn't want her to ask him where Joe was. He would have liked to go into the living room to watch the game with Pat and Jack, but he was afraid the men would question him about his studying. He slipped quietly out of the kitchen and up to his room. Perhaps nobody would notice that Joe had not come.

In his room he was faced with a dilemma. He really could study by himself, of course. But if Joe wasn't keeping his bargain, why should he? It wouldn't be fair if Joe watched the game and he, Tomasito, had to sit there all evening and struggle with homework. Besides, it would be embarrassing if he had been good when his friend had been bad.

Tomasito didn't dare watch the game on TV, but he could listen to it on the little radio Jack had given him. The more he thought of this possibility, the more tempting it became. He got the radio out of his desk drawer and attached the earphone.

"And show me what you did on Saturday," requested Miss Ramirez on Monday night as she went over the week's work. The boys turned pale and began looking at the floor.

Finally, Joe spoke. "Saturday night the Giants broke their tie with the Dodgers. I just had to watch, Miss Ramirez. It was such an important game."

147

Miss Ramirez was silent for a second or two. "And you, Tomasito Chavez?" she asked.

Tomasito could not remember his English. "*Yo también, señorita,*" he stammered, his voice quivering. "I am sorry."

Again there was silence. The boys felt as though an electric charge were building up. They looked cautiously at Miss Ramirez. Suddenly she got up from her chair and began to pace back and forth.

"So!" she said at last, stopping at the table where the boys sat. "I give up my precious Monday evenings to give you lazy boys a chance. You made a bargain—and what happens? You break your contract just to watch some grownup children playing ball!" Miss Ramirez didn't shout. On the contrary, her voice remained low and ladylike. But she spat out her words like ammunition and the boys felt as if they were being hit with buckshot.

"I don't know what to do," Miss Ramirez went on, tossing back her shiny black hair and rapping the heels of her white pumps on the floor. "It's just no use working with boys who would give up their future for a ball game!"

Fear made Tomasito's muscles stiff and he ached with shame. At the same time, as he watched Miss Ramirez out of the corner of his eye, some part of his mind began to think, "When she's angry, she's almost as pretty as Teresa."

At last the teacher's wrath seemed to exhaust itself. She sat down at the table and asked, in a milder tone, "What shall we do, boys? As you know, I have asked the school principal for a special favor for you. If I were to assure him that you could succeed in eighth grade and then you let me down, that would be pretty bad, wouldn't it? The principal wouldn't think much of me as a teacher."

This last statement struck home. "We are really sorry, Miss

148

Ramirez," Tomasito quavered. "Please forgive us. We won't fail you again."

"To make up, we will prove to you," volunteered Joe, "that we can work by ourselves. There are only two weeks of summer left. Tommy and I will work without you, and on the Monday before Labor Day you can give us an exam to see if we are ready for eighth grade. You'll do that, won't you, Tom?"

"Oh, yes!" agreed Tomasito. "Please, Miss Ramirez, let us show you what we can do."

Miss Ramirez smiled at last and held out her hands to the boys. "That's the spirit! Now, if you can do that—all by yourselves—I will be proud to have you in my class."

The boys stuck to their bargain. Every night immediately after dinner they went to work on their books. It wasn't easy. There were many tourists now and they were tired from the work on the llama rides. But they were better at studying. They knew how to go about it now and they could help each other.

Tomasito had confessed their Saturday night defection to Teresa and she had apparently told Jack. Nobody mentioned Miss Ramirez' absence on Monday night. The boys studied together all evening. It seemed to Tomasito that Jack was especially companionable at breakfast next morning.

"It's a good thing you made me pay attention to the meadow hay last year, Tommy," he observed. "It was great not to have to worry about fodder all last winter. But it's lucky I got Phil to mow the hay by machine this year. The way you and Joe are hitting those books, you would never have had time for haying!"

"I hope we make enough on the llama rides to pay for the machine, Jack," Tomasito replied.

"Oh, you made enough last winter at the resort to pay for that," Jack reassured him.

Tomasito beamed. Now if he could only pass that exam!

The day for the examination finally arrived. Tomasito and Joe were allowed to close the llama rides early so that they could wash and change before going over to the school. Miss Ramirez had arranged for them to take their exam in the eighth-grade classroom. They were to be there at seven and Teresa gave both boys an early supper. She drove them to the school herself.

On the way the boys said not a word. It seemed to them as if every piece of knowledge they possessed had vanished from their minds.

They knocked on the classroom door and Miss Ramirez called to them to enter. She was sitting at her desk, looking as crisp and pretty as ever. Beside her sat the school principal. The boys turned pale.

"Sit down in the middle row, boys," Miss Ramirez said cheerfully. "I know you are surprised to see Mr. Thomas here, but don't be nervous. I am so proud of what you have done this summer that I want him to see for himself what progress you have made. Mr. Thomas, you know Tommy Chavez and Joe Henry. You will learn that they are ready for eighth grade."

"Miss Ramirez tells me you have worked very hard, boys," the principal said. "I didn't think you could do all those back lessons in one summer—"

"You will see that they have," Miss Ramirez interrupted quickly.

The examination began, the first part being oral. In his nervousness Tomasito was afraid he might reply to the questions in Spanish or in Quechua. But Miss Ramirez started off with such easy things that the boys couldn't fail to answer correctly and soon they forgot themselves and began to take pride in showing what they knew. As the questions became harder and they continued to know most of the answers, Miss Ramirez' black eyes began to sparkle and Mr. Thomas began to nod his head in approval.

Next came arithmetic problems which they did on paper; then Miss Ramirez had them write a short English composition.

"Now for the final questions," she said solemnly when they had finished. "Tomasito, what is the principal habitat of the llama? And Joe, who is ahead, the Giants or the Dodgers?"

The boys could not help smiling and Mr. Thomas laughed aloud.

"You may go outside for a few minutes, boys. Mr. Thomas and I will look over your papers," Miss Ramirez said then. "We will call you back just as quickly as possible."

Stiffly, Tomasito and Joe moved outdoors. The sunset still glowed in the sky. Teresa was sitting in one of the swings on the playground, talking to Uncle Joe and Sam Henry. Joe's mother was there and so was Jack.

"All over?" Jack asked, as he saw the boys.

"They're correcting the papers," Tomasito answered numbly.

"Come in, boys." Miss Ramirez finally called from the doorway. "The rest of you come too," she said, beckoning.

They all filed in, silent and tense. "Sit down," invited the teacher. "Mr. Thomas, please tell the boys the results of their examination."

"Young men," began the principal solemnly, "I am happy to announce that you have passed your special examination in

151

a very creditable manner. You have proved to Miss Ramirez and to me that you are ready to enter eighth grade. I hereby award you certificates of promotion." He handed each boy a card. They managed to thank him with words as well as with beaming smiles. Tomasito started to say, "*Gracias, señor,*" but remembered his English just in time.

There were congratulations all around and everyone was invited to come back to Teresa's kitchen for hot chocolate and cookies.

"You boys deserve a holiday," announced Jack during the celebration. "Next weekend Johnnie and Sharon, with a little help from the rest of us, can run the rides with just two llamas and the burros. You two can take Allca and Quilla and go on a camping trip—that is, if Sam will let Joe go."

Before the boys could express their delight, Uncle Joe broke in. "What I want to know is what *my* reward will be if I am as good a pupil of Miss Ramirez as you boys were."

"Before you start talking of rewards," Miss Ramirez retorted, "just remember that the boys left their teacher behind and earned their victory by themselves."

It was another golden autumn. The sky was the same piercing blue as it had been last year and the sunlight was just as dazzling. The school bus made its daily rounds and the boys took the llamas climbing after school. It was the same as last year—and yet how different! School again, but what a change here, too. The boys could hardly believe how much they had learned during those summer evenings. They really could do eighth-grade work. When Miss Ramirez called on them in class they could usually answer the questions correctly. This amazed them almost as much as it did their fellow students.

To his surprise, Tomasito found that he could write Eng-

152

lish readily enough. Miss Ramirez assured him that there was nothing magic about this. "Look at all the writing you did during the summer," she reminded him.

Not that school was easy. Miss Ramirez made everybody work very hard, especially Joe and Tomasito—or so they thought. There were many times when the boys wished they could go back to former days of leisure, to TV and football. They complained to Miss Ramirez that they had no time for fun.

"You worked all day during the summer and made up a whole year of school work in the evenings. If you could do that, you should be able to plan for fun, too," she told them. And she gave them several suggestions about budgeting their time.

"Aren't you two lonesome for seventh grade?" teased Uncle Joe.

In the regular Sunday afternoon football scrimmages, Tomasito was discovering that he could now hold his own.

"Your brother Pablo would be surprised to see you playing American football," observed Jack.

"Peruvians can play anything," bragged Tomasito.

Uncle Joe didn't go to Sacramento after all. He stayed in Parson's Flat and set up a small law office in a unit of the Sierra Motel as well as one in South Tahoe. He spent three days a week in each place. "Teacher told me to," he explained to the boys, laughingly. He kept books for the resort and did a few other odd jobs as well, in order to earn a living. When election time came around in November, he ran for County Clerk instead of Supervisor. He still didn't win, but he got many more votes than in June.

"Mr. Joe Henry," wrote the editor of the *Muir County Herald,* "is showing promise as a local politician. Perhaps it is

153

because, as our first local lawyer, he has shown that he is interested in the affairs of his fellow citizens."

"Aren't you proud of your pupil?" Uncle Joe asked Miss Ramirez.

"Are you going to run for Supervisor in the spring?" Tomasito wanted to know.

"I think it will take quite a few years to build up my political career to that point," confessed Uncle Joe. "But if the Wilson River floods again this spring, I'll sure sue the government!"

The Christmas season arrived and this year Tomasito had many good things to write home. He knew that the best gift he could send would be the news of his success in school. He was almost beginning to forget how to write Spanish, but Miss Ramirez knew the language and helped correct his letter to Don Pedro. Proudly Tomasito told his old friend how much he had enjoyed reading *The Incas*—in English!

Don Pedro had not forgotten his young protegé. He sent Tomasito a long letter telling of the new diggings, some of them sponsored by the United Nations. "How we need you, my son," he wrote. "We cannot get enough young men with knowledge and patience to put together the pieces of the past."

Tomasito took special pleasure in sending word to Papá that the little herd of llamas was doing well in California. Even in the winter the llamas were earning him his board and room.

Quilla was soon to have another kid. Everyone hoped that this time all would go well. It was a milder winter and Quilla was now used to the change of seasons. To be on the safe side, Tomasito asked Jack to let him consult with a veterinarian. None of the local vets had ever doctored a llama, or even a camel, but Tomasito felt better after he had talked to him.

"No doubt it was the infection," the vet said, after listening to the account of Quilla's illness. "And the sulfa pills probably cured her. But maybe that Indian tea helped too. Anyhow, here's a supply of antibiotics for emergencies. Call me if you need help."

Fortunately, Quilla had no trouble when her time came. Her pure-black kid was born quickly and soon bobbed and pranced beside her mother in the corral and up the mountain paths.

"Since her mother is Quilla, the Moon," suggested Teresa, "let us call her Tuta, the Night."

"I wish we hadn't promised to send her to the San Francisco Zoo," sighed Tomasito. "Now she will turn to gold."

Teresa, who did not know of Tomasito's fearful dream, answered smilingly, "Well, yes, my brother. With the gold she brings, you will be able to study and to go back to Don Pedro."

Teresa, now an experienced wife and mother, was at home in her new land and Tomasito rejoiced that she too had found fulfillment and happiness. Little Paul was more than a year old now. Try as he would, Tomasito still found his deep feeling of dislike for the child to be the one unresolved problem in his otherwise shiny new life. He sincerely tried to love the little boy, but whenever he looked at the shattered pieces of the sacred clay llama, he felt bitter toward Paul. This made him feel guilty, for how could a baby help what he did? And did it really matter? Don Pedro would surely forgive the accident. But the sight of the broken llama always brought to Tomasito chill memories of last year's broken hopes.

155

One day near Easter Sharon brought Paul a plaster bunny as a present. It was not long until Paul, in his eagerness to carry it, dropped the toy and broke it.

"Tommy and Johnnie," begged Teresa, "please walk down to Sorenson's for me and get some of that glue it tells about on TV. It's supposed to fix anything. Perhaps we can glue the rabbit together before Sharon sees it. Then she won't be disappointed."

The rabbit was soon back together again. Tomasito suddenly thought of Don Pedro's words. "We cannot get enough young men with knowledge and patience to put together the pieces of the past."

"My sister," he said to Teresa in Quechua. "May I have the rest of the glue? I have an important task."

Teresa gave him the glue, but she could see that she should not ask what it was for. Every morning, for several days after that, she heard the alarm ring in Tomasito's room a half hour early. When she asked her brother why he rose so early, he replied, "I have work to do, my sister."

On Easter morning, after various ceremonies, both North and South American, Tomasito said to Teresa, "Come to my room, my sister. I have a surprise for you."

In his room, Tomasito went to his desk. From the desk drawer he brought forth a little package wrapped in tissue paper.

"This is for Paul," he said. "You can keep it for him till he's older." Teresa unwrapped the object. It was the ancient charm, the Inca llama which Don Pedro had given him, whole and perfect again.

"But my brother! A miracle! And for Paul!"

"No, it's not a miracle. This is my work. Don Pedro told me that only the very patient ones can put together the pieces of

156

the past. Now I know that I am such a one. And now I would like to give the llama to Paul. Some day, when he is a grown man, *he* can take it back to Peru where it belongs."

"Oh, my brother," cried Teresa. "Already you are like Don Pedro. Now the little llama can remind Paul of our strong and patient men of Peru—of the Incas and of Don Pedro—and of Papá and of you. Thank you, thank you, my brother!"